Not Just Any Earl

ANNA BRADLEY

OLIVER
HEBER
BOOKS

CHAPTER
ONE

HAMBLEDEN MANOR,
BUCKINGHAMSHIRE, ENGLAND, MAY, 1812

" I f I didn't know it to be impossible, Emmeline Templeton, I'd think you were burying bodies back there."

Emmeline startled, then smothered a yelp at the sudden, sharp sting in her thumb.

Drat. Cursed thorns.

She caught the drop of blood on the tip of her tongue and scrambled to her feet, her lips curving in a grin when she saw Lady Fosberry standing on the other side of the rusted iron gate that surrounded the walled garden. "Perhaps I am burying bodies. How can you be so certain it *is* impossible?"

"Because there isn't a spare body to be had within two counties of Hambleden Manor." Lady Fosberry waved a hand at the deserted garden before turning her attention back to Emmeline, a disapproving frown on her lips. "Come out from behind that shrub at once, and let me see the worst of it. Do you suppose you can hide from me?"

Emmeline *had* supposed so, but she should have known better. Lady Fosberry could spot the flutter of a butterfly's wings from miles away. "I beg your pardon, my lady." Emmeline made a futile attempt to brush off the dirt smearing her pinafore. "If I'd known you intended a visit today, I would have made myself presentable."

"My dear child, we both know that to be an egregious lie." Lady Fosberry took in Emmeline's unruly hair and muddy boots with a despairing shake of her head. "You're an utter fright, just as I suspected. You must stop digging in the dirt in this outrageous way, Emmeline. Young ladies shouldn't behave like common laborers. It's unbecoming."

As she was the only one who ever labored in the walled garden since they'd lost their groundskeeper two years earlier, Emmeline supposed she was common enough, and it wasn't as if there was anyone about to see her.

No one ever came to Hambleden Manor anymore.

Emmeline couldn't imagine why Lady Fosberry still bothered with them, but she'd been a dear friend of their father's, and had proved a steadfast friend since scandal chased the Templetons out of London three years earlier.

"I just popped in to have a look at my father's roses." *What's left of them.* Neglect and disease had reduced what was once a blooming garden to a few sickly canes and a handful of withered leaves. "It's dirty work, I'm afraid."

Lady Fosberry's face softened at the mention of James Templeton. "You're a good girl, Emmeline, for all your odd ways."

Emmeline smiled at that. Lady Fosberry would think her even odder if she knew Emmeline had been digging in the dirt beneath her father's roses for most of the afternoon, and enjoying every muddy, thorny moment of it. "I'm surprised to see you, my lady. We didn't expect you in Buckinghamshire until the season ended."

"What, and let Helena leave without bidding her goodbye? No, indeed."

Emmeline's smile faded. Her younger sister Helena was leaving Hambleden Manor in a few days to take up a new position as a governess with an acquaintance of Lady Fosberry's, and there was no telling when the five of them would all be together again.

If ever.

Their futures looked grim, indeed. What had once been a handsome fortune had dwindled to nothing. One by one, they'd all be forced out to work, and their beloved home would fall prey to decay until there was nothing left—

"I've brought a dozen of Helena's favorite teacakes from London, with Cook's compliments, and of course she'll have my coach for the journey, with two of my footmen."

"You're very good, my lady," Emmeline murmured past the lump in her throat.

"Nonsense." Lady Fosberry waved aside her own kindness, as she always did. "Quickly, now, dearest. There's a juicy tidbit in *The Times*, and a devilish bit of nonsense in *The Morning Post* I'm certain you'll find diverting."

Emmeline never found gossiping diverting, but she allowed herself to be dragged inside, where she deposited Lady Fosberry in the drawing room, then dashed upstairs to tidy herself. By the time she returned all four of her sisters were there, with the eldest, Euphemia, in her usual place in front of the fireplace.

"Emmeline, here you are at last! Goodness, that took an age. Come here, child, and sit by me." Lady Fosberry patted the empty space beside her on the settee. "Now, shall we see what wicked gossip *The Times* has for us today?"

"Yes, yes!" Mathilda, the youngest of them all at age sixteen, let out an excited squeal as Lady Fosberry handed her the paper.

"Is it terribly wicked?" Juliet, who was seated on the other side of Emmeline tried to read the print over Tilly's shoulder. "What is it, Tilly?"

Tilly scanned the paper, then passed it to Juliet with a disappointed sigh. "It's not at all wicked."

"Well, what fun is that?" Juliet read the page, then handed it to Helena with a shrug. "It seems Lord Boggs has made a certain lady an offer of marriage, and she's declined him. They don't mention the lady's name."

"Ah, but I happen to know the lady's name." Lady Fosberry waggled her brows. "I had it from an unimpeachable source, I assure you."

None of them even thought to question the reliability of these unimpeachable sources. The Countess of Fosberry had the ear of the Upper Ten Thousand. For all her kindness, her ladyship was an incurable gossip, and never missed a tidbit.

"Shall we see if you all can guess which lady has ruined Lord Boggs's fondest hopes?"

"Lady Mariana Shelby," Emmeline said, before any of her sisters could utter a word.

Lady Fosberry clapped, delighted. "Remarkable, Emmeline! Really, you girls are a wonder. I begin to suspect you're all hiding crystal balls under your beds."

"There's not a bit of magic to it," Phee protested. "It's simply—"

"Mathematics, or some such nonsense." Lady Fosberry flapped her hand, as if banishing mathematics from her presence. "Yes, you've said so before, Euphemia, and it's a clever theory, but mathematics teaches us nothing whatsoever about love."

"It's not really mathematics, my lady, so much as predictable patterns. As children we do learn from mathematics how to recognize patterns by studying numbers in a sequence, but—"

"People aren't numbers, Euphemia," Lady Fosberry interrupted. "I hope you'll all find out the truth of my words for yourselves, before it's too late."

It's already too late for us.

The words rose unbidden in Emmeline's mind, but she said only, "Tilly may, one day."

By the time Tilly was old enough to marry, maybe the *ton* would have forgiven the Templeton sisters for their mother's sins.

"You see, my lady, Lord Boggs has previously demonstrated a weakness for a pretty face." Phee, undeterred by Lady Fosberry's scold, was warming to her subject. "It only makes sense he'd offer for the prettiest lady this season, because he does so every year. One can anticipate, within reason, his future behavior by his past actions."

"If it's as simple as you say, Euphemia, then what is Lord Boggs's trouble? Why hasn't he found a willing lady to marry him yet?"

"Lord Boggs's trouble," Helena said, "Is that he

wants a young lady of both beauty *and* fortune, but he can't lure one into marriage because he's—"

"Not at all handsome. He's old, very ugly, and unpleasant, too, and Lady Mariana is—"

"Tilly!" Emmeline cried. "Shame on you!"

"Lady Mariana's father is a viscount, and she's very pretty," Tilly went on, ignoring Emmeline. "She needn't marry a fortune, and Lord Boggs's only attraction is his fortune. He needs a lady who hasn't two shillings to rub together."

"Yes, but he *is* an earl, Tilly." Helena tossed the newspaper aside. "Given that the *ton* only cares about titles and fortunes, one would think Lord Boggs might have whomever he chooses."

"He doesn't *want* just anyone. He wants a belle." Emmeline thought for a moment. "Miss Crowley would do for him. She's not a great beauty like Lady Mariana, but she's pretty, and as poor as a rookeries' church mouse."

Juliet helped herself to one of Helena's teacakes. "Lady Mariana has been holding out for Mr. Mayhew, but the season is half over already, and—"

"And a bird in the hand, you know." Helena grinned. "For my part, I'd much rather see Lady Mariana with Mr. Mayhew, but Lord Mayhew despises Lord Shelby, and Mr. Mayhew won't disoblige his uncle, or he'll be cut off without a shilling."

"Yes, and that will never do for a gentleman who plays as deep as Mr. Mayhew. There's another pattern for you, my lady." Phee turned to Lady Fosberry with a provoking grin. "All the Mayhew men are hardened gamesters, and they all marry fortunes. I predict Mr. Mayhew will offer for Lady Philippa Wingate."

"I don't like to see poor Miss Crowley get stuck

with Lord Boggs." Helena let out a little sigh on behalf of poor Miss Crowley. "He's two decades older than she is!"

"Yes, but it would be an excellent match for her. Not a happy one, but secure, certainly." Juliet finished her teacake and dusted the crumbs from her fingers. "Don't you think so, Lady Fosberry?"

"The match has merit from Miss Crowley's perspective, yes, but I've never liked such matches. It seems a shame to condemn such a sweet young lady as Miss Crowley to a lifetime with demanding, ill-tempered Lord Boggs."

"It's wrong we should know so much about a gentleman we've never met." Helena wrinkled her nose. "Gossip is a dreadful thing!"

"Dreadful! Why, I think it's perfectly delightful! But my dears, what do you say to this?" Lady Fosberry paused until she had their full attention. "I have it on the highest authority Lord Melrose intends to marry this season."

"Lord Melrose! Isn't he the...what do you call it?" Tilly's brows drew together. "I can't remember what one is meant to call a gentleman who's an Incomparable."

"The Nonesuch," Helena said. "One refers to him as the Nonesuch."

"No, one refers to him as *Lord Melrose*." Juliet fell back against the sofa, feigning a swoon.

Emmeline rolled her eyes. "Lord Melrose was meant to marry last season, as well, and the season before that. The *ton* always thinks he's steps away from stumbling into the parson's mousetrap, but he hasn't been caught yet."

It didn't appear to Emmeline that Lord Melrose

was in any hurry to marry, but Lady Fosberry was never wrong about such things. If she said Lord Melrose would wed this season, the man was doomed to become betrothed before grouse season commenced.

"I think he'll offer for Lady Philippa."

Lady Fosberry attempted a careless shrug, but Emmeline didn't miss the mischievous gleam in her ladyship's eyes, and she hid a smile. Her ladyship was forever trying to trip them into a matchmaking error, but she was rarely successful. "Lord Melrose is meant to marry Lady Christine Dingley. His mother wished for the match, and he's hardly going to go against his deceased mother's wishes, is he?"

"Besides, Lady Christine is the season's belle," Juliet added. "To the belle go the spoils."

Emmeline thought the marriage mart was rather ridiculous, really, with its belle, and the Incomparable, and the Nonesuch. But then the *ton* was ridiculous.

Why would their approach to marriage be sensible?

"I can't say I think Lord Melrose is the sort to defy expectations." Phee tapped her lip, considering it. "Particularly in a matter of such consequence as choosing a wife."

"He *is* very proper," Helena agreed.

"Well, he's had to be since that awful fever took his parents off. Dreadful business, that." Lady Fosberry shuddered. "An ancient title, an enormous fortune, a dozen or more properties, and three younger sisters to look after knocked the boyish antics right out of poor Melrose."

"But even his mistresses are proper." Tilly

snatched another teacake off the plate. "Let's not forget his mistresses."

"Tilly!" Emmeline scolded, shocked. "Hush, will you?"

"What, do you suppose I don't know about mistresses? Well, I do. Lord Melrose has had a number of them, and each of them as proper as a governess."

"Is there such a thing as a proper mistress?" Juliet turned a doubtful look on Lady Fosberry.

Lady Fosberry gave an airy wave of her hand. "Discreet widows are the thing."

"Never mind his mistresses." Emmeline shot Tilly a quelling look. "If past patterns are predictive of future behavior, and I submit they *are*—"

"Predictive behavioral patterns." Lady Fosberry snorted. "My dear girl, people are nothing if not *un*predictable. They rarely do what one expects them to. You'd do well to remember that."

"—Lord Melrose will do precisely what's expected of him, and marry Lady Christine," Emmeline finished.

"He hasn't yet. Indeed, he doesn't appear to have the least inclination toward Lady Christine, and the season is nearly half finished. The *ton* begins to whisper she won't bring him up to scratch." Lady Fosberry lowered her voice, as if Lady Christine's failure were shocking, indeed.

"That *is* curious." That Lord Melrose hadn't yet succumbed to Lady Christine's dubious charms rather improved him in Emmeline's estimation, but she predicted his rebellion would be short-lived.

"Still, there must be something to your theories," Lady Fosberry admitted grudgingly. "You did predict Lord Eaton would marry Miss Yates last season, though it was her third season and the *ton* had given her up as a spinster."

"One needn't have a comprehensive knowledge of mathematics to put Lord Eaton and Miss Yates together. He's wanted her since her first season, and was only waiting for his father to die before offering for her."

Still, Emmeline couldn't deny she and her sisters *had* been remarkably accurate, for all that their matchmaking had begun as a game. It was meant to be a harmless way for them to amuse themselves, but they'd honed their skills over the long, quiet winters in Buckinghamshire.

"As for Lord Melrose, you forget, my dears, that I've known him since he was in short pants. I tell you, he's just the gentleman to surprise us all."

"I'll allow it's statistically *possible*—" Phee began.

"As are many things that will *never* happen," Emmeline interrupted.

"—but given Lord Melrose's behavioral patterns, I don't think it likely. I predict Lady Christine will become the Countess of Melrose before the final ball of the season."

Emmeline thought it rather a pity, really, as she didn't think Lord Melrose and Lady Christine a good match, but then everyone paid a price for the gifts bestowed upon them by fate, and Lord Melrose appeared destined to be cursed with a silly, disagreeable wife.

"Oh, that reminds me!" Lady Fosberry snatched up the copy of *The Morning Gazette* she'd brought with her this afternoon. "There's the most delectable bit of gossip here about Lady Philippa nearly coming to blows with Lady Christine over a length of lavender silk at Madame Toussaint's shop."

Emmeline couldn't imagine an existence where a length of lavender silk was one's greatest concern. "Who won the prize? Lady Christine, or Lady Philippa?"

"Lady Christine." Lady Fosberry's brow furrowed. "I can't make out how she did it, as she's a dainty little thing, but then a lady is known to find great reserves of strength when it comes to a pretty piece of silk."

"If Lady Christine has chosen lavender," Tilly observed, "It must be all the rage this season."

"Indeed, my dears, there's not a single scrap of lavender silk to be had in all of London."

"*Lavender*, of all absurd colors." Juliet began on another teacake. "It doesn't flatter any but the fairest ladies, but then I suppose that's why Lady Christine chose it."

"Lady Christine's machinations will serve her well this season." Helena nibbled daintily around the edges of her own teacake, a thoughtful expression on her face. "The marriage mart is rather like the animal kingdom, isn't it? The most aggressive members of the herd flourish, while—"

"*Herd?*" Lady Fosberry gasped. "I'm going to act as if I didn't hear that, Helena Templeton."

"The difference is, animals act by instinct alone, whereas the *ton* is motivated by cultural prejudices, social pressure, and economic gain. It's perfectly logical in a civilized society to approach marriage thus, of course, but—"

"Love isn't logical, Emmeline!" Lady Fosberry

gave an offended sniff. "Neither is the heart a civilized organ, nor should it be!"

"Are we talking about love?" Helena asked innocently. "I thought we were discussing *marriage*."

"My dear child, one hopes they're one and the same."

"You misunderstand me, my lady. I mean to say the *ton* would do better to approach marriage with an eye to complementary characteristics, rather than fortune and pedigree, but they limit themselves by choosing spouses only from their own exalted ranks. I don't have anything to say against love." Emmeline had nothing to say in favor of it, either, but she thought it prudent to keep that opinion to herself.

"Humph. Well, I'm pleased to hear you say so, as cynicism is *not* an attractive quality in a young lady."

Was she cynical? Emmeline didn't think so, though perhaps her own disastrous season had jaded her somewhat. Above all, though, she was a *scientist*. "When one considers the matter scientifically, matchmaking isn't so very different from botany."

"Not botany again!" Tilly buried her face in her hands with a groan.

Emmeline ignored her. "A mindful botanist doesn't just cobble together any two roses that happen to grow in the same garden and expect a perfect bloom. They research a plant's characteristics, study their growth patterns, then choose two that are ideally matched, plant them in fertile soil, and nurture them until the desired outcome is achieved."

"Well then, girls." Lady Fosberry looked between them, a calculating gleam in her eyes. "Since you're all such accomplished matchmakers, who would you all choose for Lord Melrose? Who is his ideal match?"

"A lady from this season's offerings, you mean?" Emmeline asked.

"No, I mean any lady, *ton* or not, and regardless of her family or fortune."

"I'd choose a lady who is fond of the country, but equally at home in London," Phee said. "A lady who delights in society, but who values family above all else. A lady of beauty, wit, and spirit. A lady of charm and vivacity, with some experience of grief to lend depth to her character, but who hasn't been irretrievably damaged by it."

Lady Fosberry arched a brow. "My goodness, Euphemia, you seem to have given Lord Melrose's marriage prospects a great deal of thought. Who, may I inquire, is this paragon of womanhood?"

"A lady very much like..." Phee paused dramatically. "Miss Juliet Templeton."

There was a brief, stunned silence, and then the room exploded in excited chatter.

"Juliet! Well, she is the prettiest lady I know. Much prettier than Lady Mariana," Tilly declared, with a fond glance at Juliet.

"Certainly, she's the only one of us with any pretensions to being a beauty." Helena studied Juliet for a moment, then gave a decisive nod. "Yes, I think you'd do very well as the Countess of Melrose."

Juliet and Lord Melrose? Emmeline cocked her head, considering it.

If there'd been another lady to rival Juliet among the ranks of the *ton*, Emmeline would have despaired of her sister having any chance at all with Lord Melrose, but his options this season were disappointingly few. The young ladies on offer were very much in the style of Lady Christine.

Lord Melrose didn't strike Emmeline as the sort of gentleman to surprise them, no matter what Lady Fosberry said. Still, if he *were* willing to choose a bride from outside the aristocracy, he'd likely gravitate toward a lady like Juliet, for all the reasons Phee had mentioned.

That was a significant *if*, however.

While an animal would naturally choose their best mate when presented with them, gentlemen, alas, weren't as clever as animals. Lord Melrose might be predisposed to choose a mate with Juliet's characteristics, but first he'd have to abandon all the criteria by which aristocratic gentlemen chose their spouses.

Emmeline had yet to see *that* happen.

Juliet seemed to agree, because she was gaping at her sisters as if they'd all gone mad. "The Countess of Melrose! I have as much chance of becoming a countess as I do a turnip. I don't even *know* Lord Melrose, and short of his having a carriage accident outside Hambleden Manor, I daresay I never will."

Helena deflated. "That is a bit of a stumbling block, isn't it?"

"Oh, but there isn't any reason you can't meet him." Lady Fosberry made a great show of smoothing her skirts. "Unless, of course, you're not as certain of your matchmaking schemes as you profess to be."

Emmeline frowned. "What do you mean?"

"It's quite simple, really. If you're as confident as you say you are, then you won't object to testing your theories, will you? Isn't that what scientists do?"

Emmeline exchanged a glance with Phee. "Yes, but how are we meant to test such a thing? Present Juliet to Lord Melrose on a silver platter as if she was a teacake, and inform him she's his future countess?"

Lady Fosberry snorted. "I wouldn't go that far. No, I'm merely suggesting a tiny wager, that's all."

Emmeline didn't like the sound of that, nor did she trust the shrewd glint in Lady Fosberry's eyes. "What sort of wager?"

"Why, only this, dearest. You'll come to London with me when I return tomorrow, and apply your matchmaking schemes to the marriage mart."

Emmeline's eyes went wide.

No, surely not. Surely, she couldn't be serious—

"I'll go!" Tilly cried, bouncing on her chair with excitement. "Please, may I go, Phee?"

Phee was staring at Lady Fosberry, all the color gone from her cheeks.

"Phee? Mayn't I—"

"*No*, Tilly." Phee's tone was harsher than usual. "You're far too young for a London season."

"Emmeline and Juliet, then." But Lady Fosberry's gaze was fixed on Emmeline. "If your theories prove accurate, and Juliet receives an offer from Lord Melrose, I'll take Euphemia to the Continent with me this winter, and give Tilly a season when the time comes."

Emmeline's mouth dropped open. "But that's...*no*, my lady. You're very generous, but we can't possibly do such a thing."

It was one thing for them to speculate about *ton* matches amongst themselves, and quite another to engage in callous, unfeeling wagers about the lives of real people.

Even callous, unfeeling people.

"Well, that *is* disappointing," Lady Fosberry said with a sigh. "Is there nothing I can say to persuade you?"

"No." Emmeline shook her head. "Not a single thing. I'm afraid it's out of the question, my lady."

"Pity." Lady Fosberry plucked a bit of lint from her sleeve. "Did I mention, Emmeline, that my rose garden flourishes? No? I daresay I forgot to tell you that your dear papa gifted me with ever so many cuttings from his rare hybrid roses."

Emmeline stared at her, speechless.

Why, Lady Fosberry might have been Eve herself, but in place of an apple, she was holding the promise of a deep, red rose in her hand.

Dear God, the woman was positively diabolical.

Lady Fosberry knew how badly Emmeline wanted to save her father's beloved roses, particularly the "Hambleden Glory," a truly exceptional specimen he'd named to honor the home he'd loved so well.

She had plans for that rose, plans she hadn't shared with anyone.

But a season in London? The very idea was appalling.

Emmeline opened her mouth to refuse again, but before she could utter a word, Juliet stunned them all by rising to her feet and declaring, in a tone that discouraged any argument, "I accept your wager, Lady Fosberry. When do we leave for London?"

CHAPTER
TWO

HAMPSTEAD HEATH, LONDON, ONE
MONTH LATER

J ohnathan Parrish—the celebrated Earl of
Melrose, the gentleman the young ladies sighed
over, the Nonesuch, the Corinthian, the petted
and admired darling of the *ton*—was two fingers
of brandy away from casting up his accounts all over
Lady Fosberry's gleaming ballroom floor.

He couldn't be certain, not being a man who usually drank to excess, but Johnathan had a vague notion casting up one's accounts during a cotillion
wasn't the done thing.

The devil of it was, he couldn't work out how the
evening had disintegrated into a drunken debauch.
He and Lord Cross had set out with the intention of
going directly to Lady Fosberry's ball, but one glass of
brandy in Cross's study had led to another, then another, and then somehow, they'd ended up at
White's.

It went a bit hazy after that, but now Lady Fosberry's ballroom was spinning around Johnathan in a
nauseating whirl of gold damask wallpaper.

"We would have done better to avoid this ball al-
together, Melrose."

17

Johnathan peered at Lord Cross. He didn't seem to be in the least impaired by the brandy, but then those weaknesses that afflicted mere mortal men—drunkenness, lust, love—never had much effect on him.

Cross was scrutinizing the company with his usual expression—one eyebrow quirked, jaw relaxed, and infinitesimal crinkles at the corners of his eyes. "How in the world do you do that, Cross?"

The eyebrow rose a notch. "Do what?"

Johnathan waved a hand at Cross's face. "Contrive to look both bored and amused at the same time. I've always wondered."

Cross rolled his eyes. "My advice to you, Melrose, is to quit this ball before your senses quit you. I don't know what's come over you this evening, but you're in no state of mind for a cotillion."

Johnathan drew himself up with as much dignity as he could muster, given his difficulties with the gold wallpaper. "Are you implying I can't hold my drink? How dare you, Cross?"

"Did I *imply* it? I didn't suppose I'd been that subtle. You've dipped too deep tonight, Melrose, and you're too bloody foxed to take your lady out to the floor. Is that plain enough for you?"

Johnathan grunted. "You're an unpleasant fellow, Cross. I don't know why I insisted on having your company this season."

"I haven't the faintest idea, but I wish you hadn't."

"And she isn't *my* lady. She's *a* lady, but not *mine*." Nor would she ever be, in spite of what the *ton* might think.

Johnathan followed Lady Christine Dingley's slender figure as she tripped gracefully through a country dance. She was wearing a pastel gown of some indeterminate pale purple shade, and appeared perfectly comfortable despite the excruciating heat. There wasn't a hint of a flush on those delicate pink cheeks, or a glimmer of dampness on that smooth brow.

In a fit of misguided gallantry, Johnathan had engaged her for a dance this evening when they'd met at Lady Ponsonby's breakfast yesterday, and it was too late to beg off now.

"Save your dance with Lady Christine for another ball, Melrose."

"There won't be any other balls for me. I leave for Kent at the end of this week." Johnathan had been wishing himself anywhere but London since his first night at Almack's, and it had only grown more tiresome since then. He was eager to leave the city behind, and join his sisters at his country estate.

"If you insist, but I'm warning you, Melrose, you're sure to make a mess of it."

"Am I still standing upright, Cross?"

"For the most part. Tell me, how many noses do I have?"

Johnathan squinted at Cross. "One, er...one and a half."

Cross shrugged. "Eh, close enough."

"Well, then, let's get this over with."

The *ton* would be highly offended to hear him speak so dismissively of the season's belle. Johnathan himself was horrified. He was a gentleman, after all.

At least he would be horrified, if he were sober.

It was just that he was so *weary*.

Weary of the weight of the *ton*'s expectations, of balls and routs and breakfasts, and the throng of young ladies in their pastel gowns, with their sharp-eyed mamas scouring every ballroom for stray fortunes and titles.

On his worst days, Johnathan was weary even of being the Earl of Melrose.

It was a wearying business, being Lord Melrose. He'd been Lord Melrose for eleven years now, since he'd turned eighteen, and he was ready to drop with exhaustion.

Being Lord Melrose hadn't left him time for much else. His wild oats had been left to squirm around inside him, unsown and simmering like a pot on the boil, just waiting for their chance to overflow.

Or perhaps that was the brandy.

But of all the things that wearied him, Lady Christine Dingley was the most wearisome of them all.

Johnathan's mother had been dear friends with Lady Dingley, and it had been her fondest wish that he would one day marry her daughter. Johnathan hadn't had any objection when *one day* was a point in the far distant future, but somehow, when he wasn't paying attention, one day had become *today*.

Lady Christine had not improved in the intervening years between their last meeting and the start of this season, and Johnathan liked to think his lovely, kind mother wouldn't wish to see her only son doomed to a lifetime with an ill-tempered, spoiled belle whose only interests were shopping, gossip, and petty rivalries.

Of course, as far as the *ton* was concerned, there wasn't a single thing wrong with Lady Christine. She was beautiful, accomplished, and her family's reputation and lineage were both impeccable. That she was rather like a cricket game—that is, far pleasanter in theory than in practice—did not, in the opinion of the *ton*, disqualify her from becoming the Countess of Melrose. It did, however, disqualify her from becoming Johnathan's *wife*, which was damned inconvenient, given they were one and the same thing.

He'd already made up his mind to wed this year. He'd just turned twenty-nine, and Margaret, the eldest of his three younger sisters was now fifteen years of age. She'd abandoned her pinafores and youthful curls, and soon enough would be embarking on her first season, with her younger sisters right behind her.

He needed a wife.

The devil of it was, marriage had always meant Lady Christine Dingley, or, if not *her*, then another lady very much like her.

Hence, the brandy.

Just once, he longed for something for *himself*, something he'd *chosen*, instead of having it thrust upon him. Something, or someone, that was *his* alone—

"If you want this dance, Melrose, you might endeavor to look as if you're anticipating a cotillion, rather than a trip to the gallows."

Johnathan shot a resentful look at Cross. "Yes, all right. I'm going."

"Get on with it, then." Cross plucked at his wilted cravat. "I've never seen such a crush, and it's as hot as Hades in here."

"It's always hotter than Hades in a ballroom, Cross, and every ball is a crush. Must the *ton* always move in a herd? Aren't there any other entertainments on offer tonight?"

"Certainly, but none so fashionable as this one,

and none with such an enticing hint of scandal about it."

Johnathan frowned. "Scandal? What scandal?"

"Haven't you heard, Melrose? Lady Fosberry has dragged one of the Templeton sisters back from the dead."

"Not from the *dead*, Cross. Only from Buckinghamshire. Lady Fosberry spends a good deal of time at her country estate there. What, are people still going on about the Templeton girls? It's not their fault their mother was an adventuress, and ran off to the Continent with the Marquess of Bromley."

"No, but the mother is dead now, Melrose, and someone must be blamed, or else the *ton* won't be satisfied, and so it falls on the daughters. Lady Fosberry and her misfits." Cross's mouth turned up in a rare smile.

"Lady Fosberry has always cared more for intrigue than propriety." The *ton* flocked to her balls for that very reason. One never knew what might happen at one of Lady Fosberry's entertainments.

"Quickly, Melrose, before some gallant steals Lady Christine out from under your nose." Cross nodded toward the other side of the ballroom, where Lord Cudworth, Lady Christine's last partner had just returned her to her parents. "I refuse to wait through another interminable country dance."

Johnathan's lips twisted in a grimace, but he gave the hem of his coat a sharp tug, resisted the urge to twitch the folds of his cravat, and began to make his way across the ballroom.

If he'd had one fewer glasses of brandy, or been a trifle less agitated he might have arrived at his destination, but as it was, he never made it as far as Lady Christine.

Instead, he spied Lady Susanna Exeter, a discreet but delectable widow with whom he'd enjoyed more than one pleasurable encounter. Indeed, if he hadn't made up his mind to wed this season, he'd still be enjoying her *now*.

Johnathan glanced from Lady Susanna to Lady Christine, then back again. Once, twice, then again, back and forth, one lady a reminder of a recent, pleasurable past, and the other a thorn in the side of his filial duty.

He took a hesitant step toward Lady Christine, his mother's wishes regarding his marriage battering at his bruised conscience, but then paused, his gaze wandering back to Lady Susanna.

Surely his mother hadn't meant for him to be made miserable by his choice? She couldn't have known her dear friend Lady Dingley would raise such a foolish, frivolous, ungrateful daughter who, despite the *ton*'s approval, was as ill-suited to become the Countess of Melrose as a feral cat?

Good Lord, he *was* in a mood. Hardly the right frame of mind for a cotillion, was it?

Johnathan's heated gaze roved over Lady Susanna, taking in the dark, shiny curls gathered into an elegant knot at the back of her head, several long locks of which had been left loose to caress what looked like acres of smooth, white bosom, presented to great advantage by a tight bodice of dark pink silk.

Cross had been right all along. Johnathan *was* too deep in his cups, and it *would* have been best if they'd avoided this ball entirely, but it was difficult to care, now he had Lady Susanna in his sights.

Besides, Lady Christine's dance card was likely full for the evening. Yes, of course it would be. She *was* the belle. Mystifying, that, in much the same way cricket being one of England's most beloved sports was mystifying.

Johnathan prowled through the crowd, his gaze on those dark curls, that white bosom, but he was sluggish from drink, and everywhere he turned he found a wall of bodies blocking his way.

By the time he made it to Lady Susanna's corner, she'd vanished.

Damnation. Where could she have gone in the time it took him to cross a ballroom?

He turned this way and that, frowning at the faces swimming around him, but the silky curls and generous bosom were nowhere to be seen. He huffed out a breath, and was about to return to Cross, admit defeat, and allow his friend to take him home when he spied a darkened hallway adjacent to the alcove where Lady Susanna had been standing.

He stepped closer and peered into the gloom. Perhaps she'd gone...ah, yes! Just there, a fold of pink silk, whisking around the corner.

Later, Johnathan would pinpoint that fateful moment as the one in which his better angels abandoned him.

~

EMMELINE TIPTOED THROUGH THE GARDEN, the rich scent of soil and roses teasing her nose.

Seventeen, eighteen, nineteen, and...yes, just there!

At the very end of the very last row, where it

might bathe in the full heat and light of the afternoon sun, was the Hambleden Glory, her father's prized hybrid, the one she'd feared was lost forever.

She squeezed her eyes closed, but it was too late. Tears—*tears*, of all absurd things—were stinging her nose, threatening to spill down her cheeks. Emmeline swiped her hand across her eyes, impatient with herself.

This was no time for tears.

She was meant to be tucked safely inside her bedchamber, not running about the gardens at night with her hair in a wild tangle and nothing but a pair of flimsy silk slippers on her feet, but the roses were most fragrant at night, before their oils evaporated in the sun.

Not that it would matter to Lady Fosberry if she happened to wander onto one of the balconies off the drawing room and catch sight of Emmeline out here. She'd find herself in a carriage on her way back to Buckinghamshire before the sun rose tomorrow morning.

At any other time, an escape from London would be a reason to rejoice, but that was before Emmeline had found the Hambleden Glory.

It wasn't in bloom yet. The buds were still tightly furled, protecting the delicate treasure inside. Emmeline had only ever seen it in bloom once, in the walled garden at home, but she'd known it the moment she saw it tonight by its distinctive, glossy green leaves and the elongated shape of the rosebuds.

It was a big, extravagant rose with sprawling scarlet blooms, the dramatic color a perfect match for an exotic, complex scent that was difficult to describe, but that made Emmeline think of cloves, violets, and honeysuckle.

If ever a rose were destined to become a perfume, it was the Hambleden Glory.

Her father had known it, had recognized it at once, and begun distilling the scent in his workroom, his big, rough hands gentle on the delicate petals, careful of the oils in their dark glass bottles.

Emmeline reached into her pocket, pulled out a tiny bundle, and peeled back several layers of linen. Nestled inside was a violet ribbon, faded with time and too much handling, but a faint scent still clung to the limp silk.

It was all she had left of the scent he'd created. He'd fallen ill soon after he perfected the formula, and died soon afterwards, leaving only a tiny bottle behind with enough scent to fill the center of Emmeline's palm, but no more.

He hadn't written the formula down. He rarely did, and even if he had, Emmeline would never have been able to find it in the clutter of his workroom, but she had a nose for scent, just as her father had, and she'd managed to pinpoint the various scents in his formula.

For the most part.

The Hambleden Glory with a touch of coriander to temper the sweetness, orris root, the barest trace of plum, and...something else.

A second rose, certainly a damask, perhaps one of his rare hybrids, one with a delicate scent of ginger, but despite a frantic search through every inch of dirt in the walled garden, Emmeline hadn't found it. The elusive rose had likely fallen victim to the blight that had reduced her father's beloved rose garden to ruins.

But Lady Fosberry's garden was a different matter entirely. Surely one of the twenty thriving roses in their tidy rows would prove to be the one she needed. She'd dropped the last of the perfume left in the tiny glass bottle onto the silk ribbon to preserve the scent, and enough of it still lingered for her to identify the rose she sought in Lady Fosberry's garden by its fragrance.

If it was here.

Once she found it, she'd know it, but there was one difficulty.

Only about half of the roses in Lady Fosberry's garden were in bloom, and the rose she needed to complete the perfume wasn't among them. So, she'd have to wait and hope one of the unopened roses was the one she was searching for.

If not...well it *would* be, that was all. Surely she hadn't gotten this far for fate to cruelly disappoint her in the end? If she could only find that rose, she could recreate the perfume, and persuade one of the shops in London to sell it, just as her father had intended. It would be a fitting tribute to the father she'd adored and lost, and her final gift to him.

A single perfume wasn't likely to eradicate her family's financial difficulties, but if she could make enough to keep them all together, it would lift the great, crushing weight from her chest.

What was sneaking about a dark garden, compared to what she stood to gain? A midnight wander was harmless enough, surely? It wasn't as if anyone was going to see—

A rattling sound caught Emmeline's attention, and she jerked her head toward the drive to see yet another carriage making its way toward the glowing entrance of Lady Fosberry's estate. She stuffed the ribbon and the linen into her pocket and ducked down just in time to elude the sweep of light from the carriage lantern.

Dear God, all of London must be at Lady Fosberry's ball by now. Emmeline couldn't imagine a single ballroom could be large enough to contain them all. An image of aristocrats crawling over every available surface of Lady Fosberry's house like ants over a rotting bit of fruit rose to Emmeline's mind, and an involuntary shudder skidded down her spine.

Perhaps it was time she retired to her bedchamber.

She peeked over the top edge of the rose bush she'd darted behind, and waited until the carriage disgorged this new group of revelers—ladies this time, in silks and flashing jewels—and they vanished into the house.

Emmeline glanced down the drive, but she didn't see another carriage approaching, so she ventured forth, creeping from her hiding place among the roses to the south wing of the house. She'd done a thorough search of it this afternoon, and found a narrow passageway from the music room that was connected to a back staircase that led to her bedchamber. She could use that without having to go anywhere near the ballroom.

After all, *she* hadn't made this cursed wager, and she certainly hadn't agreed to actually *talk* to anyone. It wasn't as if *she* intended to be betrothed by the end of the season.

There was, after all, only so much science could do.

She was here for the roses, nothing more.

Well, that and to keep an eye on Juliet.

She paused when she reached the door leading from the garden terrace to the corridor beyond. The last thing she wanted was to risk running into some simpering miss, gossiping matron or arrogant lord, but all was dark and quiet.

Nearly there...

Just a quick nip into the library first to fetch the copy of Thomas Whateley's *Observations on Modern Gardening* she'd left there this afternoon, and she'd be back in her bedchamber without anyone being aware she'd ever left it.

The library door stood partially open, and the last embers of a fire were still burning in the grate. Now, where had she left Mr. Whateley? Emmeline closed the library door behind her and hurried over to the bookshelf, pressing her nose close to the spines of the books on the third shelf from the top, squinting in the gloom.

Ah, yes, there it was, just where she'd left—

Creak.

Emmeline froze at the sound of the library door opening slowly behind her.

For an instant, she had the ludicrous thought that she might duck behind the heavy silk draperies framing the window beside her before she could be seen, but that hope was shattered when a deep, disturbingly male voice murmured, "Ah, at last. I thought you'd vanished. You weren't running away from me, were you?"

A thousand different responses crowded into Emmeline's head at once—that she didn't know him, that she hadn't been running away from *him*, but from *all* of them—and nearly fell from her dazed lips before she realized he wasn't talking to *her*, but to another lady.

The one he'd mistaken her for.

It should have been simple enough then to turn around and tell him the lady he'd followed into the library had indeed run away from him, but as soon as she spoke, he'd demand to know her name, and all it would take was a single word—*Templeton*—before the gossips would gleefully pick up where they'd left off three years earlier, and she'd be caught in the midst of another nightmare.

...Templetons back in London... lured the poor man into a dark library... the daughter just like her mother...

So, Emmeline remained as she was, silent and paralyzed by indecision, her heart thrashing about like a fish on a hook, and wished with everything inside her that this gentleman would realize his mistake and be on his way.

There was a pause in which it felt as if the entire world hung suspended in a single, tense moment, followed by the soft tread of footsteps against the thick carpet, and then he was behind her, so close his warmth heated her chilled skin, his breath drifting over the back of her neck, a hint of sweet, rich brandy teasing her nose.

She sensed he would touch her before he did, felt the subtle shift in the air behind her, but his caress, when it came, wasn't anything like she'd imagined a man's touch would be.

Fingertips curled against her waist, his large hands so gentle she might have believed she'd imagined the caress if she hadn't felt the brush of his coat sleeves against her wrists and looked down to find long, gloved fingers resting on her hips.

Then, before she could move or say a word, he buried his face in her hair.

It was so unexpected, so unbearably sweet, Emmeline's limbs went heavy and liquid, and a sound fell from her lips, a sound she couldn't recall ever having made before, or could even have imagined making before this man touched her.

She swayed against him, instinctively seeking more of his gentle caress. A low, pleased sound rumbled in his chest, and firm, soft lips pressed against the sensitive skin of her neck, behind her ear, and then his teeth—*his teeth*—were nibbling at her earlobe.

Dear God, how could anything feel as good as that?

He took his time, exploring every inch of the untouched terrain of her neck before his parted lips drifted lower to taste the top of her spine, the light rasp of an emerging beard on his cheeks and jaw making her shiver.

Emmeline reached out to grip the windowsill, to anchor herself against the strange, hot ache unfurling inside her. In some distant, hazy part of her mind she was aware it was madness, utter madness to permit an unknown gentleman to touch her so intimately, but his wandering lips scattered her wits, and stole her reason.

He urged her closer, one hand flattening against her hip while the other ventured higher, pausing to stroke the slight swell of her belly before gliding over her ribs, and then his warm palm curved loosely around her throat, the gentle pressure of his fingertips against her jaw easing her head to one side and baring the curve where her neck met her shoulder to his kiss, the damp tease of his tongue.

Emmeline's eyes slid closed, and whatever vague thoughts she'd had of escaping him fluttered away on a breathless sigh, like clouds on a summer breeze.

CHAPTER
THREE

The room was dark, and she was half-hidden behind the heavy silk draperies, but she was wearing a pink silk...well, it was *some* color of a gown. Johnathan couldn't quite tell what color, the world having gone a bit fuzzy at the edges, but it must be pink, mustn't it?

"This gown suits you," he whispered against her skin, reaching out to stroke one of her long curls. "That shade brings out the rich color of your hair."

She stiffened, and he paused for an instant, confused, but after a moment the tension eased from her slender frame, and the long, white fingers clutching the edge of the windowsill relaxed.

What had become of her gloves?

The thought was there and then gone again as he buried his face in the impossibly soft skin of her neck. "Dear God, you smell divine." He opened his lips over the pulse behind her ear, groaning at the seductive scent. It was soft, with a subtle hint of roses, but it was earthy, as well, like rich soil and clean skin warmed by the sun. "Is this a new perfume? You should never wear any other."

He gathered up the long, luscious curl he'd loosened from where it had fallen against her pale neck, captured it between his fingers, and raised it to his mouth. She made a sound, a sharp intake of breath. Desire flooded his belly as he dragged the silky strands across his lips, and then he was lost in her seductive scent.

A quiet sigh left her lips, a slow, sweet exhale unlike any he'd ever heard from her before, and arousal shot through him, headier and more dizzying than the brandy he'd consumed. He wrapped his hands around her slender waist and eased her back against him, and she...

For one strange, frozen moment it felt to Johnathan as if she was about to pull away from him. He wanted her badly, but he loosened his hold on her waist at once.

He might be deep in his cups, but he wasn't a brute.

But she didn't pull away. Instead, she arched into him, one hand stealing up to cradle the back of his neck, her fingers sifting through his hair.

"*Yes.*" Johnathan's heavy eyelids dropped closed, and he eased her hips back, tucking the tantalizing warmth of her against him, so she could feel how much he wanted her.

He'd admired Lady Susanna from the first moment he'd seen her, had desired her, but this time his passion for her felt different, deeper, a needy ache not just in his cock, but everywhere, in his palms that throbbed to cradle her breasts, in his fingertips and his lips, the arch of his neck clamoring for her touch, his mouth desperate for her tongue.

Christ, even the soles of his feet wanted her.

Everywhere, every inch of him was desperate to have her, but this wasn't his bedchamber, and several hundred people were crowded together just at the other end of the hallway.

A gentleman didn't toss up a lady's skirts in his hostess's library.

"My carriage is just outside," he murmured, unable to resist the temptation to nip at the dainty lobe of her ear. "Will you come with me?"

No answer, unless it was the maddening drift of her fingers over the back of his neck. Johnathan groaned, every hair rising in reaction to her touch.

But a gentleman didn't toss up a lady's skirts...

She turned her head, and her soft breath drifted over his jaw.

A gentleman didn't toss up...

He trailed his fingertips over the slender curves of her hips, across her belly, and the sound she made, that needy little gasp, God *help* him.

This is a library, and not even your library.

It's Lady...Lady...Lady Somebody-or-Other's library.

Johnathan let his fingers wander higher, tracing a line from her belly to the space between her breasts, praying for strength when he found her unencumbered by a corset, all her delicious curves unbound, as if she'd been waiting for the stroke of his roving hands.

No corset? That didn't seem—

She caught his hand and pressed her lips to his palm.

A gentleman didn't toss...

No matter how much he wanted her. No matter that he was trembling for her, his cock as rigid as an iron spike, pressing against his breeches, his chest heaving with every labored breath, his head swimming—

A gentleman didn't...

But Johnathan did. He *was*.

He wrapped a hand in her hair and eased her head back, swallowing at the sight of the long, graceful curve of her neck laid out like a feast before him. He caught her chin between gentle fingertips and turned her head aside so he could press his lips there, his tongue darting out to taste the arch between her neck and shoulder, his hands sliding up to cradle her breasts.

A soft cry fell from her lips as he stroked her, the peaks of her nipples going taut against his palms, and just like that, with her hungry little pleas echoing in his head, Johnathan was lost, his hand fisting her skirt and dragging it to her knees, then higher, imagining the pink silk caressing her thighs, and higher still, past the warm, wet hollow between her legs where he was dying to bury his face, his mouth, his tongue. "I want to taste you, Susanna."

She went utterly still, her reaction so sudden and unexpected it chased some of the fog of desire from Johnathan's head. "Susanna? It's all right, sweetheart. It's Melrose."

A gasp broke from her lips, shattering the quiet. It was a gasp of distress, not passion, and in one baffling instant, she went rigid against him. Johnathan froze, stunned. "Susanna? I beg your—"

But she didn't give him a chance to beg for anything. Before he could utter another word, she snatched her skirt from his fist, jerked it down, and tore herself from his arms.

Johnathan instinctively moved to follow her, to catch her and soothe her with whispered assurances, but she was gone in a whirl of skirts, leaving behind only the memory of her silky hair against his lips, and a faint scent of roses.

He stood there for long, silent moments, dazed, but the lady had made her choice. There was nothing left for him to do but return to the ballroom.

Johnathan gathered himself together, his heart curiously heavy in his chest, but just as he was leaving the library, he stepped on something, and leaned down to pluck it up.

It was a violet ribbon.

He pressed the smooth silk to his nose, and drew in a deep breath.

Roses.

He slipped the ribbon into his pocket, and left the library.

LATER, Emmeline wouldn't recall how she managed to gather her wits enough to tear herself from his arms at last, nor would she remember her frantic flight down the corridor, a prayer on her lips that she wouldn't meet anyone else—dear God, *please*—her feet echoing on the bare wooden boards of the staircase, then the blur of figured green damask wallpaper in the hallway on the third floor.

Then, at last, the safety of her bedchamber, her lungs on fire, her breath ragged, tearing at her throat as she sucked in great gulps of air.

It's all right, sweetheart. It's Melrose.

There was only one Lord Melrose in London, and

he was the very same Lord Melrose Juliet had wagered on, the same Lord Melrose who was meant to make Juliet his countess before the end of the season!

Emmeline's head met the door behind her with a hard thump.

No, it can't be. I can't possibly be so unlucky as to—

"Emmeline, is that you? Oh, thank goodness! Where have you been? Help me loosen some of these buttons, will you?"

Emmeline stared dumbly at Juliet, uncomprehending, her heart still pounding.

"Emmeline! Quickly, dearest, before I collapse."

Juliet was tearing at the neckline of her gown, panting, her cheeks flushed with hectic color. Emmeline, recalled to her senses, turned Juliet around and began attacking the long row of silk-covered buttons on the back of the gown. "I told you this gown was too tight, Juliet!"

"It wasn't too tight yesterday." Juliet was still trying to catch her breath.

Emmeline wrestled with the delicate violet silk until at last she managed to loosen a half-dozen buttons. "You didn't consume four cream cakes at tea yesterday, as you did today. Dash it, these buttons are as slippery as those treacherous satin slippers you're wearing. I'm shocked you didn't turn an ankle."

"The heat nearly finished me, if that gratifies you. The corset, too, please. Oh, I wish I could do without one, as you do!"

"I wasn't graced with your curves." Nor would she have known what to do with them if she had been.

Once she'd freed Juliet from the gown and corset, her sister fell onto the bed with a theatrical flop. "Thank goodness! You've no idea what a narrow escape I've had, but I simply *refuse* to swoon at my first ball of my very first season."

"It's fashionable to swoon." Emmeline leaned over the bed, flapping Whateley's *Observations on Modern Gardening*—which she'd somehow miraculously held onto during her encounter with Lord Melrose—in front of Juliet's face to cool her.

"If one is a delicate, tender young lady in modest ivory silk, which I most decidedly am not." Juliet plucked fretfully at her damp cotton shift. "Oh, dear. I'm all sticky."

Emmeline peered down at Juliet's face, an anxious frown on her lips. "Why didn't you call a servant to help you unlace?"

"I expected you'd be here, and I thought once I'd caught my breath, I might go back down."

"You can't go back down, Juliet. Indeed, there's no question of it. You're far too warm, and you don't look well. I advise you to go to bed at once."

"But I haven't danced with Lord Melrose yet! How am I meant to marry the man and win our wager with Lady Fosberry if I never even dance with him?"

Warmth seared Emmeline's cheeks at the mention of Lord Melrose. The better question was, how was Lord Melrose meant to dance with Juliet when he was kissing Emmeline in Lady Fosberry's library?

Dear God, what have I done?

"There will be other balls," she managed to choke out.

"Yes, you're right. I'm wrung out, I'm afraid." Juliet pushed a straggling lock of hair from her forehead, and grimaced at her wrinkled gown. "Where did you run off to, Emmeline? I thought you meant to remain in your bedchamber all evening."

"I was just...er, I was..."

Kissing Lord Melrose in the library. Yes, the same Lord Melrose you're meant to be betrothed to by the end of the season, only it wasn't just kissing, there was touching, too, and—

Juliet's eyes narrowed on her face. "Why are you so flushed and out of breath?"

"Flushed?" Emmeline gulped. "Who's flushed? Not me, I assure—"

"Never mind," Juliet said, waving a hand. "I know where you've been."

"You *do*?" Emmeline's voice was little more than a panicked squeak.

"Of course." Juliet gave her a puzzled look. "You've been down in Lady Fosberry's rose garden, haven't you?"

"*Yes*. Yes, indeed, I have!" It wasn't a lie, after all.

"I do wish you'd changed your mind about attending the ball tonight, Emmeline. You will come to the next one, won't you? You're such a graceful dancer."

Emmeline recognized Juliet's best wheedling tone, and let out an inelegant snort.

"You can't come to London for a season and refuse to dance a single dance, Emmeline."

"I can, quite happily, and anyway, I don't imagine the circumstances of my not dancing would have changed if I *had* gone to the ballroom."

"Nonsense. I'm sure you would have had a perfectly lovely time."

Certainly, if one could call an evening spent among the *ton* lovely, which Emmeline did *not*. "Never mind me. I'm content as I am. Now, off to bed with you."

The sooner Emmeline put this day behind her, the better.

But Lord Melrose refused to be dismissed as easily at that. He haunted the darkest hours of the night, his low, deep whisper in her ear, his soft lips leaving trails of fire across her skin, his quickened breath and the gentle rasp of his beard awakening nerve endings she didn't even know she possessed, despite her diligent study of human physiology.

She danced along the edge between dreams and memories until light began to peek around the closed draperies. It was only then Emmeline realized she'd left the linen bundle with her ribbon inside stuffed into the pocket of her dress.

She eased the coverlet aside, careful not to disturb her sleeping sister, and tiptoed across the floor to her discarded gown. She searched through the pockets, a relieved breath leaving her lungs when she felt the rough texture of linen under her fingertips.

But her relief was short-lived. The bundle was open, the layers of linen crumpled, and her violet ribbon...

It was gone. Her ribbon was gone.

CHAPTER
FOUR

"Tell me once again what we're doing here, Cross?"

Johnathan rubbed his aching temples, and prayed his skull would have the decency to wait until he returned home before it exploded. He hadn't ventured out at all today, and now he was regretting allowing Cross to talk him into a meal at White's.

White's, of all places. The scene of last night's crime.

Last night's *first* crime, that is. Johnathan vaguely recalled there'd been another. The details of it were hazy, his only clue the violet ribbon he'd been clutching in his hand when he awoke this morning.

Cross didn't appear to hear him. "Why is everyone gaping at us, Melrose?"

"No one's gaping at us." Johnathan passed a weary hand over his stinging eyes. "You're imagining it."

"The entire dining room is watching our every move, Melrose. Or rather, *your* every move."

"They're not staring at *me*."

Cross glanced around the dining room, his dark

brows lowered. "The devil they're not. Those fools at Lord Quigley's table have been gawking and sniggering at you like a troop of chattering monkeys since the moment we sat down."

Johnathan lifted his head. "A troop? Is that what a group of monkeys is called?"

Cross scowled. "I believe you've missed my point. I'm telling you, Melrose, something is off. There's a wager afoot, and I fancy it has to do with you. What in the blazes did you get up to at Lady Fosberry's ball last night? Do you even remember? I've never seen you so deep in your cups—"

"What do you take me for, Cross? Of course, I remember." Johnathan pinched the bridge of his nose. Good Lord, even his nostrils hurt. "Most of it, at any rate." Cross raised a skeptical eyebrow, and Johnathan let out an impatient sigh. "Oh, all right. Very little of it, if you must know."

"That's what I thought." Cross set aside his fork, rose to his feet, and went to consult the betting book. He was there for some time, turning over page after page. His face remained carefully blank as he made his way back to the table with every eye in the room upon him, but his cheeks had gone white.

"For God's sake, Melrose," Cross hissed as he took his seat. "Were you trifling with some chit in Lady Fosberry's library last night?"

There *had* been a library. Johnathan was certain of that much. Logic would suggest it had been Lady Fosberry's library. As for the chit...

"Not some chit, Cross. Lady Exeter."

"Whoever you were debauching, it wasn't Lady Exeter. I saw her leave with Lord Pemberton not five minutes after you left me to go dance with Lady Christine."

"I'm certain it was Lady Exeter I followed into—" Johnathan broke off, falling silent as snatches of conversation reached him from every corner of the dining room.

"...wouldn't be Lady Exeter's first indiscretion with Melrose, but her gown was pink, not purple."

"Purple?" Johnathan met Cross's eyes. "What bloody purple gown?"

"Cudworth said the gown was *lavender*, not purple." Lord Quigley was several tables away, but his booming voice easily carried across the dining room. "He saw the girl fleeing Lady Fosberry's library himself, but it was too dark to see her face."

Johnathan froze. *Cudworth.* He might have known. If ever there was a man with a knack for being in the very last place one wanted to find him, it was Cudworth.

"I have twenty guineas here that says Lord Dingley challenges Melrose to a duel over this." A florid-faced man at another table shot Lord Quigley an infuriating smirk. "What say you, Quigley?"

"Dingley's not such a fool as that." Lord Quigley gave a comfortable laugh. "Melrose will put a ball in him before Dingley's finger can twitch on the trigger. I'll lay you twenty guineas it was Lady Christine Dingley in that library with Melrose. That's one way to bring him up to scratch, eh?"

Johnathan started to rise to his feet, anger coursing through him. He had no love for Lady Christine, but he wouldn't sit here silently and let Quigley malign her.

Before he could strangle Quigley, however, Cross

stopped him with a hand on his arm. "Don't, Melrose. It will be taken as confirmation of the rumor, and make things worse."

Johnathan sank back into his seat and stared at his friend, aghast. "Good Lord, Cross. What have I done?"

Cross gave him a helpless shrug, and Johnathan let his head sink into his hands.

The better question was, what *hadn't* he done? It was all coming back to him now—the spinning ballroom, the nauseating gold wallpaper, Lady Susanna's white bosom, the chase across the ballroom, and the delirious, heated moments in the library with a lady whose voice he hadn't heard, and face he hadn't seen.

Good Lord, how lowering to find all it took to turn him into an utter scoundrel was a few glasses of brandy!

"Quigley won't be the only one wagering, Melrose." Cross kept his voice to a murmur, so only Johnathan could hear him. "There are pages of wagers in the betting book already, and the rest of London will know of it before this afternoon. What in God's name were you *thinking*?"

"Magenta," Johnathan said, stupidly enough, but for some reason, it was the only word that came to his mind just then.

Cross stared at him. "What?"

"Lady Susanna's gown. It wasn't pink, it was magenta."

"It wasn't Lady Susanna, Melrose. I told you, I saw her leave the ballroom."

Now that his head wasn't muddled with brandy and the dizzying scent of sunshine and roses, Johnathan couldn't imagine how he could ever have mistaken the lady from last night for Lady Susanna. There'd been a dozen tiny clues—the missing gloves, the lack of a corset—but even putting those details aside, hadn't he been aware, at least on a primal level, that he wasn't kissing and caressing Lady Susanna?

He had, after all, kissed Lady Susanna before, and never felt the wild surge of desire he had last night, when he'd held the mysterious lady in his arms.

Her seductive scent was both familiar and wholly unique at once. Rose, yes, but not like any rose he'd ever smelled before. It wasn't a heavy, sweet scent, like so many rose perfumes, but different somehow, though he couldn't say how, precisely. Only that it was like the difference between a perfume and a living, breathing, blooming spray of rose blossoms.

Beyond that, he couldn't be certain of anything.

"Who is she, Melrose?"

"I, ah...I haven't the faintest idea." Johnathan blanched at the expression on Cross's face. "I thought I'd followed Lady Susanna into the library, but it, ah... it seems I was mistaken."

"You were mistaken," Cross repeated flatly. "Devil of a thing to be mistaken about, Melrose."

Johnathan hardly heard him. The lady he'd kissed last night, the elusive lady in lavender—he was sure he'd never met her before. That skin he'd caressed, it had been smooth, flawless, and her hair was thick, the loose waves drifting through his fingers.

And her figure...

Dear God, her figure.

Johnathan closed his eyes as a bolt of heat arrowed down to his groin.

She was slender, her curves slight but perfectly proportioned, and they fit his hands as if she'd been sculpted just for him. If he'd ever been introduced to such a lady as *that*, he'd remember her.

Cross nudged him. "Are you all right, Melrose? You look as if you're in pain."

"The lady, Cross. I'm certain I've never been introduced to her before. She's new to London. How many petite ladies in lavender gowns could have been at Lady Fosberry's ball last night?"

"You've just described half the young ladies who've flooded the marriage mart this season, and dozens of them were at Lady Fosberry's ball."

"Well, it wasn't Lady Christine Dingley." Johnathan was certain of that much, at least. *His* lady had the softest skin he'd ever touched, the most delectable curves he'd ever caressed, and the most intoxicating scent he'd ever had the pleasure of inhaling.

Cross frowned. "You really don't remember anything about her?"

Johnathan remembered a thousand things about her—the silk of her skin under his fingertips, the seductive caress of her silky hair against his lips, the curve of her waist giving way to the gentle swell of her hips, but short of kissing, stroking and caressing every young lady in London, he didn't see how he could...

"Her scent." Johnathan sat bolt upright in his chair, his gaze meeting Cross's. "She smells like roses."

"Roses! Half the young ladies in London smell of roses."

"No, not like this. Her scent was..." Johnathan tried to think of a way to describe it, his hands fisting at his sides in frustration as words failed him. Her scent was as elusive as the lady herself. "Different. Not like any other scent I've ever experienced."

She was different.

Johnathan flushed, thinking Cross might laugh, but he said only, "There's one person in London who can tell us something definitive about the young ladies at the ball last night. I suggest we pay a call on Lady Fosberry."

∽

A LADY COULD DO a great deal of damage with a dibbler.

Emmeline grasped the rough wooden handle with both hands and slammed the spiked end into the ground. The blow vibrated up her arms with satisfying force, but instead of a neat hole ready for planting, she found a torn bit of lavender root at her feet.

Oh, dear. She hadn't meant to do *that*.

Perhaps it was time she set the dibbler aside.

She leaned the heavy tool against the back of the walled garden where she'd found it, and plopped down beside it, her back against the stone. The trouble with this garden was there wasn't a thing to *do* in it. Not a single patch of clover to attack, or diseased cane to prune, or soil to improve. It was as flawlessly maintained as the rest of Lady Fosberry's home.

It was disconcerting, all this relentless perfection.

Emmeline let her shoulders relax against the sun-warmed stone at her back and pulled her straw gardening hat low over her brow to shade her face. For a few blessed moments she thought she might drift off to sleep, but before long her mind was racing with the same thought that had kept her awake most of the night.

Lord Melrose's kiss.

Each memory chased the next through her mind, like a dog chasing its tail. She'd asked herself dozens of times what she could have been *thinking*, letting Lord Melrose kiss her, but only one answer made sense.

She hadn't been thinking at all, which was not a thing she *ever* did.

If she *had* been thinking, the violet ribbon with her father's scent would still be in her possession. She'd searched in every place she could reasonably expect to find it—the gardens, the library, her bedchamber—but it had vanished.

She dropped her head onto her bent knees with a groan. Oh, wagers were wretched, despicable, horrible things! Even now she could hardly believe she was in London, but the Countess of Fosberry could coax the devil himself into waging a soul he didn't possess.

Her kiss with Lord Melrose had begun innocently enough—that is, as innocently as any secret, passionate kiss ever did. It was a case of mistaken identity, nothing more, but if the *ton* discovered one of the infamous Templeton sisters had been kissing the peerless Lord Melrose in Lady Fosberry's library, the avalanche of gossip would shake the foundations of London itself.

Emmeline's expectations for the season had hovered somewhere between mild unpleasantness to catastrophic disaster, and the *ton* had detected a whiff of blood in the air the instant Juliet entered the ballroom last night. The gossip had started not even fifteen minutes after she descended the staircase, the whispers as thick and dense as the London fog, with the *ton* behaving as they always did when a potential scandal was brewing.

Like rabid hounds with an injured fox between their teeth.

God knew there wasn't a family in England more scandalous than the Templetons, and there was poor Juliet in the midst of it, toying with the *ton*'s patience by playing at being a respectable young lady.

Lady Fosberry might scold all she liked about people being unpredictable, but these were all the same people Emmeline remembered from her own nightmarish season, all of them saying the same things about the Templetons in the same tones of thinly veiled delight, as if their mother's disgrace had only just happened.

There was nothing unpredictable about the *ton*. At best, they had a lengthy memory for scandal. At worst, they were cruel. One needn't look any further than her own family for proof of that.

The one pleasure she'd taken in the ball had been the few moments she'd hidden in a curtained alcove on the second floor and peeked down at Juliet as she floated through the cotillion like a graceful bird soaring through the air, her cheeks pink and her borrowed violet skirts whirling around her ankles.

Warmth had flooded Emmeline's chest at the sight of her sister's smiling face. Juliet had been born for this chance, born to grace a ballroom. The ugly gossip, the stares and whispers—none of it seemed to touch her.

But now another disastrous scandal was bearing

down on them, hurtling directly toward them like a runaway carriage, all because Emmeline hadn't put a stop to Lord Melrose's advances as soon as he'd accosted her in the library.

She kicked at a rock next to her toe and sent it skittering over the dirt.

It wasn't fair. Scandalous things weren't *supposed* to happen in libraries.

She'd ended up with far more than a copy of Thomas Whateley's *Observations on Modern Gardening*, that much was certain. Instead of advice on garden enclosures, she'd found herself in the arms of the gentleman against whom every other gentleman in London this season would be measured.

Measured, and found wanting.

If she'd been able to come up with a way to extricate herself from his embrace without revealing who she was, she would have done so at once—of *course*, she would have—but given her history with the *ton*, even the mere thought of telling him her name had chilled her to the bone.

After that, though...well, there may have been a moment or two when she'd foolishly thought it might be an interesting experiment to kiss a gentleman, and it wasn't as if she'd ever get another chance to kiss the Nonesuch.

She'd had a notion that kissing couldn't be as transporting as it was rumored to be, but then he'd stroked her hair and pressed his soft lips behind her ear, and the next thing she knew the most delicious aching heat had unfurled in her belly, and...

She'd gone a bit dizzy after that, but there had been...sensations.

The dangerous kind.

Emmeline knew all about dangerous sensations, as did anyone who'd bothered to look into human physiology. What she hadn't expected was the feelings that accompanied those sensations.

Wretched things, *feelings*, especially passionate feelings.

Nothing good would come of indulging feelings. Indeed, Emmeline would prefer not to have any at all. It had been uncontrollable passions that had led her mother to run off with her lover, leaving behind her broken husband and the five daughters she'd abandoned.

She'd ruined herself, ruined them all...

Now a few stolen kisses had led to another disastrous debacle, and here were the Templetons right in the middle of it.

Again.

Except this time, she couldn't blame her mother. This time, it was all Emmeline's fault. If they were forced to flee London once again, Juliet would lose the wager, and then what would become of them all?

What would become of Phee, who'd suffered such heartache? Phee, who'd lost everything when their season was torn to shreds, including the gentleman who'd been courting her at the time. It had been Phee who'd taken care of them since their father's death, all without uttering a word of complaint—Phee who'd held them together without ever asking for a thing for herself.

No one deserved to have her heart's desire fulfilled more than Phee.

Then there was Tilly, sweet, innocent Tilly, the only one of them who hadn't been damaged by the ruinous scandal their mother had brought down upon their heads, the only one of them who looked at the world with hope, rather than suspicion.

What was she to do? How was she meant to fix this?

Her head was so muddled she couldn't think straight, but even so, she knew there was nothing to be done, aside from making certain no one—*no one*—ever discovered it had been *her*, Emmeline Templeton, who'd kissed Lord Melrose in Lady Fosberry's library.

Whatever else happened, it *must* remain a secret.

But surely no one had seen her flee the library last night? Lady Fosberry's guests had been safely occupied in the ballroom. The corridor had been deserted, she was certain of it, and even if someone had been lurking about, they wouldn't have recognized *her*. It had been quite dark, and she hadn't appeared in the ballroom at all that evening.

She was safe, perfectly safe—

Emmeline's head popped up at the sound of a carriage coming up the drive. She rose to her feet, brushed the dirt from her skirts, and made her way back to the front of the garden, so she could peek through the gate.

As soon as she saw the crest, she froze—all but her stomach, which dropped down into her half-boots.

Oh, no. It was Lord Melrose.

Her stomach lurched upwards again, crowding into her throat.

Dear God, I'm going to be sick.

Her first instinct was to flee the walled garden and conceal herself in the wilderness on the northern side of the house, but cowardice was what had gotten her into this mess to begin with. She wasn't a naughty child fleeing an enraged parent, for pity's sake, and Lord Melrose wasn't chasing after her with a birchbark switch in his flawlessly gloved hands.

But he likely does have a walking stick...

Emmeline shoved that distressing thought aside, and tried to reason herself out of her panic. It might not even be Lord Melrose at all. She may have mistaken the crest, or perhaps he'd lent his carriage to a friend, or—

The carriage door opened. An elegant, dark-haired gentleman leapt down onto the drive, and after him a gentleman with impossibly golden hair, and impossibly broad shoulders.

Lord Cross, and Lord Melrose. There was no mistaking *them*.

Lord Cross was as solemn and unsmiling as Lady Fosberry had said he was, but Johnathan Parrish, the Earl of Melrose was simply impeccable, with his fair hair, elegant figure and exquisitely tailored clothing. Why, she could see the shine on his boots from here!

He didn't look pleased. Indeed, he looked rather grim, his fair brows lowered, his mouth turned down at the corners. Emmeline couldn't imagine what a man of so many perfections had to be discontented about, or why she was unable to tear her gaze from his face, even when he wore such a sullen expression—

For pity's sake, haven't I caused enough trouble already?

She wrapped her fingers around the wrought iron bars of the gate, her heart crowding into her throat as Watkins, Lady Fosberry's butler, responded to their summons, and ushered them inside.

Emmeline had expected Lord Melrose would be handsome—every lady in England knew *that*—but the reality of Lord Melrose was even more impressive than she'd imagined he would be, than she'd imagined *any* man ever *could* be. He was everything rumor claimed he was, only more so. His legs were longer, his figure more muscular, his hair as bright as a golden guinea under the sun.

It seemed impossible *she* could have been kissing *him* mere hours earlier.

Emmeline released her grip on the gate, retreated to the other end of the garden and pressed her back against the stone fence. She wasn't *hiding*, not really. It might feel as if she was, but she only wanted a bit of shade, and anyway, it wasn't necessary for her to hover beside the gate, where anyone could see her, particularly as there was every chance Lady Fosberry wouldn't call her in, after all.

If she wasn't called, then she needn't go.

No, she'd remain right where she was until they—

"Emmeline? Emmeline, are you here?" Juliet appeared on the pathway, a frown creasing her forehead when she saw Emmeline. "Oh, there you are. Didn't you hear me call? Lady Fosberry wants you to come to the drawing room."

Emmeline took an involuntary step backwards, but her back collided with the unyielding stone wall behind her.

There was nowhere to go, nowhere to run—

"Emmeline? What's wrong? You look as if you're going to be ill."

"I...er, nothing, only I'm not fit for a call." Emmeline gestured to her dirt-soiled pinafore and the dark

55

strands of hair straggling from the sides of her bat-tered straw bonnet. "I can't possibly—"

"I'm sorry, dearest, but Lady Fosberry says you must come at once."

Emmeline gulped, but there was nothing for it but to follow Juliet from the garden into the house. All too soon, her horrified gaze landed on the open door to the drawing room, her stomach twisting into a mass of writhing knots as deep, male voices reached them in the hallway.

"Ah, here are the young ladies." Lady Fosberry waved them into the room with a bright smile. "You must allow me to introduce my friends. This is Miss Emmeline Templeton, and her sister, Miss Juliet Templeton."

The blood rushed from Emmeline's head as both gentlemen rose politely to their feet. Would Lord Melrose recognize her as the lady he'd kissed? If so, what would he do when he saw her? What would he say?

Even more to the point, what would *she* say?

"How do you do?" Lord Cross offered them each a somber bow, his curious gaze lingering on Juliet's face.

"Miss Templeton, and Miss Juliet," Lord Melrose murmured.

Those blue, blue eyes that had coaxed a thousand yearning sighs from the lips of every young lady in London passed over Emmeline's face. He took in her features one by one—chin, mouth, nose, cheekbones—until at last his gaze found hers.

A shiver darted up Emmeline's spine, very like the one she'd felt when he'd kissed her neck last night. Every one of her nerves pulled tight, her heart crawling from her chest to lodge in her throat, but before she had a chance to think, or say a single word in reply to his greeting, his gaze passed over her without a flicker of recognition.

Emmeline stood in the middle of the drawing room, dumbfounded, as Lord Melrose turned away from her to exchange pleasantries with Lady Fosberry.

He'd just looked right at her, and then in the next breath, right *through* her, without having the least inkling *she* was the lady he'd held in his arms last night.

Of all the things Emmeline had imagined might happen, of all the things she'd thought Lord Melrose might do or say when he saw her again, it had never occurred to her he'd fail to recognize her. She'd never been the sort of lady who craved a gentleman's attention—or anyone's attention, really—but she'd never felt so thoroughly overlooked in her life.

But then what had she expected would happen? That he'd recognize her the moment he entered? That he'd whisper to her in the same soft, mesmerizing voice as he had last night? That he'd snatch her into his arms, or fall to his knees and declare his undying love for her?

What nonsense! Why, it was far better he hadn't recognized her.

Still, Emmeline took her seat without a word, numb with shock, and for a single, painful instant, she wished Lady Fosberry's settee would open up beneath her, and swallow her whole.

CHAPTER
FIVE

Emmeline Templeton had a smudge of dirt on her nose.

Not *just* her nose. Her pinafore was dusty with it, and was that...yes, there were ragged bits of some sort of plant clinging to her hems.

Johnathan cast her a surreptitious glance. She sat with her hands clenched in her lap, her head down, and she hadn't uttered a single word since she'd entered the drawing room.

He might have dismissed her as dull-witted, or a prude, but that dirt...

It threw the whole picture into disarray. What sort of young lady received a morning call dusted in dirt with bits of the garden stuck to her skirts? No lady Johnathan had ever known, but he couldn't help the twitch of his lips as he gave her another sidelong glance. Just last night he'd wished for a lady who was the opposite of Lady Christine, and it seems he'd found her.

"Well, Lord Melrose and Lord Cross. Such a lovely surprise to see you both. What brings you out to Hampstead Heath?"

Johnathan jerked his attention back to Lady Fosberry, and cleared his throat. "You've never been one to listen to gossip, my lady, but there's—"

"Nonsense. You know very well I adore gossip, my lord. Let's be honest with each other, shall we? Surely, we've been friends long enough for that."

"Very well, then. I have an, ah..." Johnathan cleared his throat a second time. "A situation on my hands."

Lady Fosberry raised an eyebrow. "Oh?"

"Yes, er...well, it seems I've...it's a bit of a delicate situation you see, but..." Good Lord, this was mortifying, and he hadn't even gotten to the worst of it yet. "There was a young lady at your ball last night in a lavender gown—I thought it was magenta, but it seems I was mistaken, and she...that is, I—"

"What Lord Melrose is trying to say, Lady Fosberry, is he shared an, ah...an amorous moment with a young lady in a lavender gown in your library last night. Lord Cudworth saw her leave, and now every scoundrel in London is wagering on her identity in the betting book at White's."

A brief, stunned silence fell as the three ladies exchanged glances, then Lady Fosberry said slowly, "Well, I can't help but be pleased *someone* is getting some use out of my library."

Cross stifled a surprised snort, but Juliet Templeton didn't appear to find any of this amusing. She stared at Johnathan, outraged. "You mean to say you *don't know who she is*?"

Johnathan's cheeks heated. "I was under the impression I was, er, bestowing my affections on another lady. A particular lady, with whom I'm well acquainted. I've since found out I was mistaken."

"Mistaken?" Juliet Templeton repeated incredulously. "My goodness, Lord Melrose, that's rather a drastic mistake."

Cross, who seemed to have forgotten he'd said the very same thing to Johnathan this morning at White's, frowned at her. "Lord Melrose is fully aware—"

"Hush, Juliet, and let Lord Melrose speak."

Johnathan turned at the soft voice. Emmeline Templeton had slid to the edge of her seat, and was watching him closely. He returned her stare, and saw that she had remarkably lovely eyes. Not gray or blue, but something in between, with a dark ring around her irises, and long, thick eyelashes. Her hair appeared to be a rich chestnut, but he couldn't be certain of the color, as it was partially obscured by a ridiculous frilly lace cap that sat slightly askew atop her head.

Johnathan frowned at the offensive cap. It was the sort spinsters wore, but Emmeline Templeton couldn't be more than twenty-two years old. She wasn't one of the silly young chits that flooded the marriage mart, but she was hardly a spinster—

"It's a sticky bit of business to be sure." Lady Fosberry was shaking her head, but she loved intrigue too well to hide her excitement entirely. "How can I help, my lord?"

There was no polite way to put it, and the sooner he got the worst of this confession behind him, the better. "I thought you could assist me in discovering the identity of the Lady in Lavender."

"Forgive me, Lord Melrose, but how is Lady Fosberry meant to help find her out?" Juliet Templeton asked. "No one saw the lady's face. Not even *you*."

Cross shifted on the settee. "I suppose that's true, Miss Templeton, if one chooses to see it in the worst possible light."

"Is there another light I'm unaware of, Lord Cross?" Juliet Templeton's voice was cool, but she seemed to find Cross amusing, judging by the slight grin playing over her lips.

Cross, who did his best never to amuse anyone, returned her grin with a thin smile. "I'd wager there are a great many things you're not—"

"Never mind, Cross." Johnathan had no patience for Cross's moods today. He turned back to Lady Fosberry, wanting this thing over with. "I hoped you might be willing to help me recall which young ladies were at your ball last night."

"Particularly those young ladies who were wearing some shade of purple," Cross added.

"Oh, dear. I'd like to help, my lord, but I'm afraid that's more difficult than you might imagine. There were several hundred people here, and more than a third of them were young ladies. Let me think." Lady Fosberry was quiet as she went over her guest list in her head. "What about Lady Maria Clarke? She seems a likely candidate."

"Lady Maria wasn't wearing lavender," Juliet Templeton observed from her place beside her sister on the settee. "Her gown was orchid."

"Orchid and lavender are the same color, Miss Juliet," Cross said, his tone curt.

Another lady might have been intimidated by such a blunt correction, but there wasn't a bit of timidity in Juliet Templeton. "I beg your pardon, Lord Cross, but orchid and lavender are as different as mauve and periwinkle—that is, not the same color at all."

"They are if you're Lord Cudworth," Cross argued. "Pink, red, purple—I'd wager they're all the same to him."

"If that's the case, we should be considering every young lady who attended the ball. I do hope you're prepared for a long afternoon, as there are at least a hundred of them."

Cross stared at her, horrified. "A *hundred*?"

"Oh, but I suppose you didn't notice that, since you didn't dance a single time last night." She meant as a rebuke for Cross's lack of gallantry at the ball, but Juliet Templeton's eyes were twinkling.

"I beg your pardon, Miss Juliet," Cross drawled, his lips twitching. "Did you wish to dance with me?"

"It wasn't Lady Maria," Johnathan interrupted, before Cross could say another word. "She's much too tall. The Lady in Lavender was petite." So petite her head fit neatly under Johnathan's chin, her soft hair tickling his jaw. "Petite, and slender."

"Petite, petite..." Lady Fosberry muttered, her brow creased.

"Lady Lavinia Hall, perhaps?" Juliet Templeton suggested. "She's a petite, dainty lady."

"No. I'm acquainted with Lady Lavinia, and have danced with her before. It wasn't her." Johnathan dragged a weary hand through his hair. It wasn't *anybody*, it seemed, but rather a figment of his imagination.

A beguiling, tantalizing figment—

"What about...oh, no, she was wearing a plum-colored gown, which is nothing like...ah, yes! I believe

I have it!" Lady Fosberry exclaimed, with a triumphant smile. "It's Mrs. Granger!"

"Mrs. *Granger*?" Cross choked out, his gaze darting to Johnathan. "She's...well, I don't think it was her. Wasn't she wearing, er...mulberry, Melrose?"

"It wasn't Mrs. Granger. The Lady in Lavender is, ah..." For the third time since he'd entered the drawing room, Johnathan was obliged to clear his throat. "An innocent."

An awkward silence followed this announcement, but a burst of scarlet flooded Emmeline Templeton's cheeks, and Johnathan's eyes narrowed.

What could be the reason for that guilty flush of color? Was she simply embarrassed at the suggestive nature of the discussion, as many young ladies might be, or was it something more? He would have given anything to know, but whatever secrets Emmeline Templeton had, she was keeping them to herself.

"Lady Sarah Ward was wearing an iris silk, and Miss Hughes a heliotrope satin," Lady Fosberry offered. "Could it have been either one of them, my lord?"

It was, alas, neither Lady Sarah nor Miss Hughes, but Johnathan couldn't explain how he knew this, or how he could fail to identify the Lady in Lavender, yet still know her every curve and the texture of every inch of her skin, as if she'd been imprinted on his fingertips.

"I'd say at least two dozen ladies were wearing purple last night. It's the fashionable color this season." Juliet turned to her sister. "What do you think, Emmeline? Two dozen, or more?"

Emmeline Templeton had said little so far, and she seemed to wish to keep it that way. "I can't say, really, as I didn't attend the ball. Have you considered, my lord, waiting for this young lady to come to you?"

"She hasn't yet. I imagine the lady is embarrassed." Johnathan certainly was.

Juliet Templeton shook her head. "Better embarrassed than ruined."

"Indeed, my dear. Surely, the lady will reveal herself in her own time? I hope so, for your sake, Lord Melrose, because if it gets about you don't know who she is, I imagine you'll find yourself burdened with too many candidates, rather than too few."

Cross nodded. "Lady Fosberry is right. Even if the lady herself doesn't come forward, then some outraged papa or hot-headed brother is sure to find you, Melrose."

"That's certainly true of Miss Hughes," Lady Fosberry said. "She has four brothers, each one more hotheaded than the last. Any one of them would be pleased to put a pistol ball into Lord Melrose if he dared insult their sister."

"Or at the very least, a fist in his face," Cross added, unhelpfully, in Johnathan's opinion.

"I'm certain she'll reveal herself eventually. It's not as if it would be unpleasant to become the Countess of Melrose. A lady might do a great deal worse than you, my lord." Juliet Templeton shot a pointed look at Cross. "A *great deal* worse."

"Yes, why not give the lady a chance to manage this her own way?" Emmeline Templeton had taken up a blue velvet pillow, and was tugging at the tassels, pulling bits out, one by one. "I can't think it's necessary for you to go to such lengths to hunt her down, my lord."

Hunt her down? What an odd choice of words. "Time is a matter of some importance here, Miss Templeton."

Juliet frowned. "Why is that, my lord?"

"Because the *ton* is sure to find out who she is," Cross said. "This is just the sort of scandal to set every tongue in London wagging, and don't forget the *ton* wanted a match between Melrose and Lady Christine Dingley. Someone must be punished for disrupting it."

"Disrupting it?" Lady Fosberry's gaze sharpened. "Do you mean to say, Lord Melrose, that you intend to *marry* the Lady in Lavender?"

Johnathan stiffened. "I'm not in the habit of ruining young ladies' reputations, my lady. I think you know me well enough to know that."

"Of course you're not. You've never been a debaucher, Melrose. Indeed, this is all so out of character for you, I hardly know what to make of it, but then people are terribly unpredictable, aren't they, Emmeline?"

Miss Templeton—*Emmeline*—let out a choked sound, and Johnathan found his unwilling gaze drawn back to her. For an instant he sat there stupidly, staring at her in silence.

She noticed his perusal, and another wave of color washed over her cheeks.

It suited her, that flush, as did the touch of pink in her cheeks from the sun.

She'd been outdoors when they arrived, mucking about in the dirt, by the looks of it. Perhaps she was a gardener, but not the sort of gardener who confined herself to wandering about the gardens with a parasol, sniffing the blooms and striving to look picturesque.

She wasn't a thing like the ladies Johnathan was accustomed to. She didn't seem to care one whit for fashion, and there wasn't a bit of flirt or simper to her. He wasn't sure what to make of her, but there was something about her face that caught his attention.

That dainty, pointed chin—

"The *ton* won't stop until they've discovered who she is," Cross was saying. "It will be far better for the lady if Lord Melrose discovers her identity before they do."

"Yes, you're quite right, of course." Lady Fosberry tapped her lip, thinking. "I can come up with a list of names for you, my lord, but it would be tremendously helpful if you could tell me anything about the lady other than the color of her gown."

"The color of the lady's gown according to Lord Cudworth," Cross muttered. "*Cudworth*, of all people, who couldn't properly identify a lavender gown if he were wearing one himself."

Lady Fosberry chuckled. "I can't disagree with you there, Lord Cross, but that only makes this more difficult. There must be something else, Lord Melrose."

Johnathan fingered the violet ribbon in his pocket, but for reasons he didn't care to examine, he wanted to keep it to himself. Fool that he was, he was possessive of the blasted ribbon, protective of it.

He'd take it to one of the perfumers, instead, and find out which scent it was. Perhaps they could be persuaded to tell him which ladies had purchased that scent recently, and he could compare their names to the young ladies on Lady Fosberry's guest list.

"Lord Melrose? Do you know the color of her hair, or her eyes?"

"I'm afraid not, my lady. The library was too dark for me to distinguish her features, and she never spoke a word."

"It sounds like quite a strange encounter, my lord," Juliet Templeton murmured.

It did, but the strangest thing about it was that it hadn't been strange at all. Her warm lips, her long fingers sifting through his hair...the rightness of it had been dizzying. "I'd know her at once if I kissed her again," Johnathan said, without thinking.

"For God's sake, Melrose."

Cross frowned, but Juliet Templeton let out a delighted laugh. "Bravo, my lord. That's the first thing you've said that moves me in your favor. But of course, Lord Cross is right. You can hardly go about kissing every young lady in London."

"No, and it's a great pity, as it would be tremendously exciting if you *did*." Lady Fosberry chortled. "You'll call on us tomorrow, Lord Melrose? I'll look over my guest list this afternoon, and should have something to report then. I can't promise it will be helpful, but I'll do my best."

Johnathan dragged his attention from Emmeline Templeton's fetching blush to Lady Fosberry. "Yes. Thank you. You're very good to help me, my lady."

"Well, well, you've always been one of my favorites, Melrose, and it *is* kind of you to entertain us all with this business with the Lady in Lavender." Lady Fosberry gave him a mischievous smile. "After all, there's nothing worse than a dull season."

Johnathan wasn't certain how to reply to that, so he merely offered the ladies a final bow and made his way out of the drawing room, with Cross right behind him.

~

"MY GOODNESS, GIRLS. SUCH A SCANDAL!" Lady Fosberry breathed, as soon as Lord Melrose and Lord Cross were gone. "Poor, dear, brave Lord Melrose."

Poor Lord Melrose, indeed.

Under cover of the blue velvet pillow in her lap, Emmeline's fingers curled into fists.

What sort of gentleman kissed a lady as Lord Melrose had kissed her, without having the faintest notion he was standing beside her *the very next morning*? The worst of it was, she couldn't even reveal what an utter scoundrel he was without giving herself away!

"I think it's all nonsense," Juliet announced. "If it was too dark for Lord Cudworth to see the lady's face as she left the library, then how could he tell the color of her gown?"

"Or be certain the gentleman he saw was Lord Melrose at all?" It had most certainly been Lord Melrose, but Emmeline was desperate to try staunch the flow of this rumor, even as she knew it was hopeless. The *ton* had it now. They wouldn't let it go until they'd squeezed every drop of blood from it.

"My dear child, no one could ever mistake Lord Melrose for another gentleman. He *is* the Nonesuch, you know."

Emmeline slumped against the settee with limbs heavy with sudden exhaustion. Dear God, what a tangle. She should have listened to Phee, and kept far away from London.

What a fool she'd been to imagine for a single instant she wouldn't be found out. The *ton* was always watching, peering around every corner, ready to snap up the latest scandal like a frog catching the tastiest flies on the tips of their tongues.

"This puts an end to our wager, my lady," Juliet observed. "Lord Melrose was quite clear about his intentions regarding the Lady in Lavender."

"Oh, bother the wager!" Lady Fosberry waved a dismissive hand. "I don't give a whit about it, and never did. I've been begging Euphemia to accompany me to the Continent for months now, and you know very well I'll insist on giving Tilly a season. The wager was simply a means to get you to London, in the hopes of improving your circumstances."

Juliet smiled. "And so, we will. There are a great many other gentlemen in London aside from Lord Melrose. Perhaps I'll marry one of them."

Lady Fosberry gave her a sharp look. "I hope you aren't referring to Lord Boggs."

"Lord Boggs!" Emmeline repeated, appalled. "What's Lord Boggs got to do with anything?"

Juliet shrugged. "A bird in the hand, as Helena says."

Emmeline stared at her. "What does *that* mean?"

Lady Fosberry grimaced. "Lord Boggs admires Juliet. Anyone who attended my ball last night could see that, but I do hope you're not encouraging him, Juliet."

"I don't see why I shouldn't. You said yourself he'd be a good match for Miss Crowley. That's even more true for me, given our mother's scandal."

"He isn't a good match for you at all, Juliet!" Emmeline was horrified by the very idea.

"Are there any dreadful scandals about Lord Boggs, my lady?" Juliet asked, ignoring Emmeline and turning instead to Lady Fosberry.

"No. He's as dull as a church sermon, but there's nothing to his credit, either." Lady Fosberry exchanged glances with Emmeline. "I agree with your sister. I think him an exceedingly bad choice, Juliet, but I don't pretend to understand all the twists and turns of your magical matchmaking formula."

"There isn't a bit of magic to it, my lady." Emmeline said automatically, but her gaze remained on Juliet, uneasiness twisting in her stomach.

"Ah, yes. I keep forgetting it's simply mathematics."

"There's a great deal more to it than *that*," Emmeline protested, unable to help herself. "If you take into account psychology, even zoology—"

"My dear Emmeline, this is no time for a discussion of zoology."

"—but I don't recall a single principle of science, mathematics, or matchmaking that argues for a match between Juliet and Lord Boggs." Emmeline took Juliet's hand. "He's not the sort of man who could ever make you happy, Juliet. Just the opposite, I'm afraid."

Juliet said nothing, but she didn't need to say a word. The truth was dawning on Emmeline with such awful clarity, she couldn't imagine how she hadn't seen it sooner.

The wager, this trip to London—it had never been about a betrothal to Lord Melrose. Juliet had leapt at the chance of a season right after they'd learned Lady Mariana Shelby had refused Lord Boggs. *He* was the reason Juliet had accepted Lady Fosberry's wager, despite it going against both Phee's and Emmeline's wishes.

Now that she considered it, Emmeline would be amazed if Juliet had ever intended to pursue Lord Melrose at all. She'd likely had Lord Boggs in mind from the start.

And it was hardly a mystery as to why.

Ruin had been creeping toward the Templetons since their father's death—slow and stealthy, but as inexorable as the tide wasting away the sand at the water's edge. They didn't speak of it, but they'd all known it was coming, even after Phee had worried herself into exhaustion trying to keep them together at Hambleden Manor. But then Helena had accepted a governess position, and there'd been no hiding from the truth any longer.

A lady with Juliet's face and charm could do very well for herself in London—with a certain kind of gentleman, that is. She was as lovely as their mother had been—the only Templeton sister who could truthfully be called a beauty—and as charming and vivacious, but without Alice Templeton's hard, brittle edges, her ruinous selfishness.

There wasn't a single doubt in Emmeline's mind Juliet would sacrifice her own happiness to save the rest of them, and save Hambleden Manor.

Dear, lovely thing.

But Lord Boggs! It was out of the question. Emmeline would never allow it, but she'd have to tread carefully. Juliet was as stubborn as the rest of them, particularly once she set her mind to a thing.

But this was no longer just about a wager. It was about Juliet's happiness.

"Well, my dears, it's been rather an exciting morning, has it not? For my part, I think we should all be thanking the Lady in Lavender for rescuing us from a dreadfully dull season."

Emmeline pressed her lips together to hold back a snort.

The Lady in Lavender, indeed.

She would *not* be revealing herself to Lord Melrose, or to anyone else. The Lady in Lavender could be made to disappear as quickly as she'd appeared, and once she was gone, the *ton* would forget about her, and so would he.

Blast Lord Cudworth, anyway. He hadn't gotten a single thing right, for pity's sake. The gown had been *amethyst*, most decidedly amethyst, and it hadn't been a *gown* at all, but a day dress. Now all of London was in an uproar over the word of a man who couldn't tell the difference between the two.

"It's not every morning one finds two such handsome, robust gentlemen in one's drawing room, is it?" Lady Fosberry rubbed her hands together with glee.

Robust. A prickling heat washed over Emmeline. Yes, Lord Melrose was that, but also...surprisingly gentle, even tender. The soft press of his lips, the teasing stroke of his fingers, his slow, deep drawl in her ear.

I want to taste you...

What had he meant by that? Emmeline had spent half the night imagining the dozens of tantalizing possibilities, but he hadn't said *only* that, had he?

No, he'd said, I want to taste you, *Susanna.*

Susanna, or, as Emmeline had learned from one of

Lady Fosberry's maids this morning, Lady Susanna Exeter. Lord Melrose must be in love with her. He'd certainly kissed her as if he was.

Except he hadn't been kissing Lady Exeter at all. He'd been kissing Emmeline, touching *Emmeline*. Surely, a man in love should have known he wasn't holding his beloved in his arms? Then again, she'd *let* him kiss her, and she'd even kissed him back, so perhaps the kissing had less to do with love than she'd always supposed.

Still, their liaison in the library couldn't have made much of an impression on Lord Melrose if he couldn't even identify whom he'd shared it with, and Emmeline wasn't such a fool as to moon over a gentleman who didn't know one lady's lips from another's. A kiss didn't count if one of the participants believed themselves to be kissing someone else at the time—

"Emmeline, did you hear me? Goodness, child, you were a thousand miles away."

No, just as far as the library. "I beg your pardon, my lady. Did you say something?"

"I did, indeed. I need a few bits and bobs from the shops, so we're off to St. James's Street, but do go and change your gown first." Lady Fosberry patted Emmeline's hand. "You mustn't wander about London looking like a street urchin, you know. This is London, not Buckinghamshire."

CHAPTER
SIX

"Yes, this will do nicely." Lord Cross paused in front of the glass windows fronting Lock's Hatters, tilting his new hat this way and that until he was satisfied with the angle.

A beaver hat, of all damnable things. Johnathan's life was in turmoil, and all Cross could think about was having a new beaver hat.

"You should purchase your own hat, Melrose. The Wellington, I think. The lower brim will help hide your face from the gossips."

Johnathan came to a dead stop in the middle of St. James's Street. "Amused, are you, Cross? Well, as long as you're entertained, I have nothing more to wish for!"

Cross gave him a guilty look. "Er, well, I wouldn't say entertained, exactly—"

"I don't understand how this happened." Johnathan trailed after Cross as they made their way back toward Johnathan's carriage on Jermyn Street. "I'm still not certain I understand what *did* happen."

He'd ruined a lady whose face he'd never seen, his name was on the lips of every gossip in London, and

Lady Christine was in such a rage she'd thrown a silver hairbrush across her bedchamber and hit her lady's maid in the forehead.

At least, according to *The Morning Post*, she had.

"It's nothing so puzzling. You're not the first gentleman to be caught in an indiscretion, but you're *Melrose*. You never do anything shocking, least of all a scandalous debauchery." Cross cocked his head, considering it. "At a *ball*, in a *library*."

"Yes, thank you for the clarification, Cross. Do you know I can count on one hand the number of indiscretions I've had since I turned of age?" Johnathan held up his hand, fingers splayed to illustrate his point. "But the instant I venture a single toe out of line, the entire Upper Ten Thousand is upon me like dozens of buzzards picking apart a carcass."

"Unfortunately, this is just the sort of scandal the *ton* delights in. It does seem rather unfair, though. I daresay it will reach equilibrium eventually, however. I've found things usually do."

Johnathan gave him a sour look. "That's philosophical of you, Cross, and like most philosophical observations, utterly useless."

"I only mean to observe that the *ton* has been waiting with bated breath for you to dip a toe into the marriage mart. Now you've ruined their hopes, it's not so surprising you find yourself at the mercy of... what did you call them?"

"Buzzards."

"Yes, that's very good, though I'd liken them to a swarm of piranhas myself. Have you ever seen piranhas strip the flesh off their prey? It's fascinating. Not that it matters," Cross added hastily, at

Johnathan's darkening scowl. "Where to now, Melrose? Shall we go to White's?"

"And listen to the likes of Lord Quigley snickering behind my back? God, no. I may never set foot inside that wretched place again."

They turned the corner, and Johnathan, who had been winding his way toward Jermyn Street, glimpsed the door of the shop he intended to visit as soon as he was rid of Cross. Dozens of jars and glass bottles were artfully arranged in the window, and above it, on a royal blue background in gold script was a single word.

Floris.

Johnathan was about to suggest Cross go on to White's without him when suddenly his friend asked, "What did you make of the Templeton sisters, Melrose?"

Johnathan glanced at him in surprise. Cross rarely showed any curiosity about anyone. "Clever, both of them. Lovely, too. If it weren't for the scandal, Juliet Templeton would be this season's belle."

Cross grunted. "She's much too pert for my liking."

"Oh, you seemed to like her well enough. It looked to me as if you admired her, however reluctantly, which is rare enough."

Cross raised an eyebrow. "On the contrary, Melrose. I admire a great many ladies, until they open their mouths."

"But Juliet Templeton has such a pretty mouth. Or are we pretending you didn't notice?"

It hadn't been Juliet Templeton who'd caught Johnathan's attention, however.

That smudge of dirt on Emmeline Templeton's nose...

There was more to that young lady than met the—

"What in the *world*...look, Melrose. Isn't that Miss Emmeline Templeton?"

Johnathan followed Cross's gaze, and his mouth dropped open. There, just emerging from a carriage was indeed a lady who looked very much like Emmeline Templeton. He watched as she closed the carriage door behind her, hurried down the street, and disappeared inside Floris.

Alone. "What the devil is she doing? Where is Lady Fosberry?"

Cross was frowning. "You don't suppose she'd allow Miss Templeton to go out alone?"

"No, Lady Fosberry knows better than that."

"Perhaps Miss Templeton is lost."

It hadn't looked like it. In fact, she'd seemed to know exactly what she was doing. Still, something was amiss. Johnathan couldn't imagine how she'd managed to escape Lady Fosberry's watchful eye, but it wouldn't do for Emmeline Templeton to wander about the streets alone. "You go ahead to White's, Cross, and check the betting book while you're there, will you? I'll see to Miss Templeton."

"Yes, all right. Come to my townhouse when you've finished." Cross doffed his new beaver hat, and went back toward St. James's Street.

Johnathan waited until his friend was out of sight, then cast a furtive glance up and down Jermyn Street. Miraculously, it was early enough that there were few people about to witness Miss Templeton's impropriety, but her luck wouldn't last.

He crossed the street and peered through the window of Floris, half-expecting to see Lady Fosberry and Juliet Templeton already inside, but there was only the shopkeeper, and one customer.

Emmeline Templeton.

A dozen different scents assailed Johnathan when he stepped inside, some heavy and cloying, others delicate and complex, but he didn't detect the Lady in Lavender's rose scent, which was proving mysteriously elusive.

"...a scent for my youngest sister, but so many of the scents are too heavy for a young girl."

She'd exchanged her dreadful lace cap for a sensible straw bonnet, and her dusty pinafore for a shapeless, dark brown cloak. Neither garment flattered her—by design, Johnathan suspected. Her clothing was meant to disguise her, so she might slip by unnoticed. Miss Emmeline Templeton might be determined to avoid attention, but it was too late for that.

He'd seen her now.

She wasn't a beauty, exactly, nor was she fashionable. Hers wasn't a face that would command the notice of every gentleman in a ballroom, but there was a lovely, winsome expressiveness there he found appealing.

Now she'd caught Johnathan's eye, she held it.

"I understand you perfectly, miss. Let's see what we can find, shall we?" The shopkeeper rummaged through some cabinets and placed an array of plain, unmarked glass bottles on the polished wooden counter. "See what you make of these." He dipped a bit of paper into one of the bottles, then held it out to her. "One like this, perhaps?"

She took it between gloved fingers, raised it to her nose and took a dainty sniff. "Parma violet, with jasmine, and just a touch of..." She brought the paper to her nose again. "Vanilla?"

"Just so!" The shopkeeper beamed, pleased. "Why, how singular. I don't know one person in a dozen who could have caught that hint of vanilla. You've got an accomplished nose, miss."

An accomplished nose? Was there such a thing?

"It *is* subtle, isn't it? Vanilla is such an over-whelming scent, too. How are they able to keep it from overpowering the other scents?"

The shopkeeper leaned over the counter and low-ered his voice, as if imparting the greatest of secrets. "Just the lightest touch of coriander tempers the sweetness."

"Does it, indeed? Why, that's ingenious, Mr. Beale," she replied with a laugh. "I wonder how they ever came up with such an idea?"

"Trial and error, miss, trial and error. The creation of a perfume is an art, you know."

"A science as well, I think. Now, this one, Mr. Beale. Bergamot. One can tell by the hint of citrus— and it's paired with..." she paused to take another sniff. "Sandalwood. I think gentlemen must appre-ciate this scent, Mr. Beale?"

Johnathan drew closer, fascinated. She had a lovely voice, very soft, and as smooth as treacle drip-ping lazily from the end of a spoon.

"Indeed, it's a favorite of the young aristocratic set, particularly viscounts, for some reason, but a great many of the finest gentlemen about town wear this scent."

"Ah, I see. I had in mind something like this for my younger sister." She dipped her gloved fingers into the reticule dangling from her wrist, and drew out...a bit of paper? Johnathan couldn't quite see it, but it looked like—

The scent of roses wafted over him as she handed the paper to Mr. Beale, making his nose twitch. That scent, it was rather like...Johnathan's eyes widened in shock.

It wasn't a bit of paper at all, but a fold of linen with a scent that, to Johnathan's untrained nose, was identical to the scent that clung to the violet ribbon folded carefully in his coat pocket.

The ribbon he'd found on the floor of Lady Fosberry's library, right after the Lady in Lavender had fled.

He stared at Emmeline Templeton, dumbfounded.

She was the Lady in Lavender? Emmeline Templeton, the meek little mouse who'd hardly said a word to him in the drawing room this morning, who hadn't betrayed with so much as a gasp or twitch that she was the lady who'd kissed him with such tantalizing enthusiasm in Lady Fosberry's library?

It didn't make sense. Of all the ladies in London, she was the last he would have suspected, the last he would have imagined capable of such consuming passion.

"...recognize the scent?" Emmeline Templeton was saying.

"Let's see, shall we?" Mr. Beale brought the square of linen to his nose and gave it an experimental sniff. "Ah, that's lovely!"

Miss Templeton beamed at him. "Do you really think so?"

"Oh, yes! I've never experienced a scent quite like

it before. It's rose, obviously, with a hint of spice, and...is that honey, do you suppose?"

"I think so, yes, and perhaps a touch of plum."

"Yes, just so! I can't pinpoint the species of rose. It's a deep, complex scent. I don't believe I've ever smelled it before, but I imagine the rose it came from is very fine."

"I thought I detected two distinct rose scents. Do you agree, Mr. Beale?"

"I do, yes. I'd guess the second rose is one of the damasks, but I couldn't say which one." Mr. Beale pressed the linen to his nose again and inhaled deeply "It's a pity the scent is so faint. I'm afraid I can't tell you much." He shook his head.

"Oh, well, perhaps the roses are rare one, and difficult to find." There was no mistaking the disappointment in Miss Templeton's voice, but she offered Mr. Beale a polite smile. "You're very good to try, Mr. Beale."

"Of course, miss. Is there anything else I can do for you?"

"Well, now you ask, can you tell me anything about the distillation process? For example, I believe I read somewhere that roses must be harvested at precisely the right time, preferably at night when the fragrance is the strongest, and distilled twice—"

Johnathan listened, fascinated as she went on for some minutes about different types of oils, fermentation, and the danger of bruising delicate rose petals. Her voice was animated, her face alight with interest, all the natural reserve he'd observed in the drawing room this morning gone, and he realized with a start that *this* was a facet of the passion he'd experienced in the library last night.

Emmeline Templeton didn't lack passion. Quite the contrary.

But she hid it, just as she did her hair under that absurd lace cap.

She and Mr. Beale went back and forth for some time, and it became clearer with every word from her lips that hers was no passing interest, nor was she a novice. The lady knew a great deal about flowers and scents, and about creating perfumes.

"Lord Melrose!" Mr. Beale had been so absorbed in the discussion he hadn't noticed Johnathan, but Johnathan had unconsciously edged closer until he was standing right behind Emmeline Templeton, and now Mr. Beale caught sight of him over her shoulder. "I beg your pardon, my lord, for keeping you waiting. How may I help?"

Emmeline Templeton whirled around, startled.

"Pardon me, madam. I didn't intend to..." Johnathan blinked down at her, feigning surprise. "Oh, Miss Templeton, is that you?"

"Er, yes. Good afternoon, Lord Melrose. How do you do?"

"Good afternoon." Johnathan made a show of glancing around the shop. "You're not here alone, are you?"

"Oh, no, my lord. I, ah...well, my sister and Lady Fosberry were with me, but Lady Quigley appeared and took them off to the linen draper around the corner."

"You mean to say I've missed Lady Quigley? What dreadful luck."

He grinned down at her, and to his delight, a shy answering smile rose to her lips. "I'm afraid so. I was meant to wait in the carriage while they finished, but then I noticed Floris was right here, and I couldn't resist a visit. They'll be quite cross with me."

"I beg your pardon, but I couldn't help over-hearing your lively discussion with Mr. Beale. You know a great deal about scent and perfumes, Miss Templeton."

Her lips turned down, as if she didn't quite like this observation. "Not at all, my lord. It's merely a diversion—"

"Oh, yes, the lady's ability to distinguish scents is quite remarkable, my lord," Mr. Beale interrupted eagerly, with an admiring look at Miss Templeton. "She's got a perfumer's innate understanding of scent."

"Does she, indeed? How singular," Johnathan murmured, his gaze resting on her face. A lady with such a...how had Mr. Beale put it?

An accomplished nose.

Accomplished enough that she could create her own scent? It certainly sounded like it to him. How curious, that a lady with such a deep understanding of flowers and fragrances should have appeared in London at precisely the same time a mysterious lady with a unique and tantalizing scent had haunted Lady Fosberry's library, there and then gone again like a wraith wrapped in lavender silk.

Johnathan's heart quickened. There was nothing he wanted more than to find the lady who'd kissed him so sweetly, but what sort of conclusions could he reasonably draw from a fold of linen? It could belong to anyone. Juliet Templeton, or another lady who'd attended last night's ball. Even Lady Fosberry—

Well, probably *not* Lady Fosberry, but how could he be certain of anything?

He hadn't gotten even a glimpse of his lady's face!

Hadn't Miss Templeton said this morning she didn't attend Lady Fosberry's ball last night? But that in itself was strange, given that the Templeton sisters were Lady Fosberry's guests. Why wouldn't she attend her hostess's ball? Even if she hadn't attended, she would certainly have been somewhere in the house.

But if she *was* the Lady in Lavender, why hadn't she owned up to it this morning? Or, if not her, then why not Lady Fosberry? He'd made his intentions regarding the Lady in Lavender perfectly clear. For all her kindness, Lady Fosberry was far too worldly to let an earl slip through her fingers, particularly an earl who'd compromised her young friend.

Compromised her, yet she'd sat there on Lady Fosberry's settee, as cool as you please, and very likely lied right to his face. Or, if not outright lied, then certainly evaded, because he was sure she knew more than she was saying.

He should be furious, even insulted, but as he gazed down at her, he found himself inexplicably and utterly charmed. There was something about Emmeline Templeton that didn't make sense, and he intended to find out what it was.

"Lord Melrose? Is there something I can fetch for you?"

Johnathan wrenched his attention away from her back to the shopkeeper. "No, thank you, Mr. Beale, but I'd be pleased to wait while you and Miss Templeton discuss distillation. Miss Templeton's knowledge about perfumes is impressive, indeed."

Emmeline Templeton's lips pinched into a stubborn line. "You're mistaken, Lord Melrose. I don't know anything more about scent than any lady who's fond of roses."

Johnathan saw his chance, and seized it. "Lady Finchley's roses are among the finest in England. I'm certain you must have visited her gardens since your arrival in London?"

"No, my lord. I'm not acquainted with Lady Finchley."

"Then you must allow me to escort you through her rose garden tomorrow. The family isn't in London for the season, but Lady Finchley is a distant cousin of mine. Her housekeeper will be pleased to allow us to visit the gardens."

If Johnathan had been a vain man, he would have been mortally offended by the horrified look that passed over Miss Templeton's face at his invitation. "That's, ah...very generous of you, Lord Melrose, but I don't think—"

"Come, Miss Templeton. Perhaps we'll find this elusive damask rose you seek for your sister's perfume."

Ah, now that got her attention. A look of such intense longing passed over her face Johnathan's chest swelled with...well, *something* in response, and whatever it was, it wasn't at all pleasant. It felt almost like—

Jealousy. For God's sake, he was *jealous* of a rose.

Still, she hesitated. "Lady Fosberry may not like it."

"Let's ask her, shall we?" Johnathan offered her his arm, nodding his thanks to Mr. Beale. "You must allow me to escort you back to your carriage in any case, Miss Templeton. I can't permit you to wander about Jermyn Street alone."

She stared at his proffered arm as if she hadn't the faintest idea what to do with it, and the awkward moment dragged on until at last her gloved fingers landed lightly on his sleeve.

As soon as they stepped out the door, they encountered Lady Fosberry and Juliet Templeton bustling down the sidewalk toward Floris. "Emmeline, thank goodness! My dear girl, where in the world did you scamper off to? You mustn't...dear me, Lord Melrose! What did you come from?"

"Good afternoon, my lady. I've just been to Floris, where I found Miss Templeton conferring with the shopkeeper on distillation techniques."

Lady Fosberry gave Emmeline a fond smile. "Yes, that sounds like her."

"I happened to see her as I passed, and didn't like her to remain unescorted."

"Well, thank goodness *someone* found her!" Lady Fosberry turned a stern look on Miss Templeton. "My dear Emmeline, you can't simply wander about wherever you like. Why, White's is just around the corner, and no doubt stuffed to the brim with drunken rakes."

Johnathan choked back a laugh. "She's perfectly safe now, my lady."

"Yes, well, you're very good to return her to us, my lord. Come along then, Emmeline. We've taken up enough of his lordship's time."

"A moment, if you would, Lady Fosberry. I beg you'll allow me and Lord Cross to escort all three of you ladies on a visit to Lady Finchley's rose garden tomorrow. Miss Templeton has already consented."

"Has she, indeed?" Juliet Templeton frowned as her gaze moved between Johnathan and her sister.

"She has. With your permission, of course, Lady Fosberry."

"Why, yes, that sounds delightful."

"Wonderful. Lord Cross and I will call for you all tomorrow afternoon, then."

"Such a wonderful treat for Emmeline! She's mad for roses, you know, and would otherwise not have a chance to see Lady Finchley's, as I'm not acquainted with her ladyship."

"It's my pleasure, Lady Fosberry." Johnathan bowed, then handed the ladies into the carriage. Once they were settled, the driver flicked the reins, and the carriage rolled down Jermyn Street and disappeared around the corner onto St. James's Street.

Johnathan watched it go, a smile hovering on his lips.

Lady Fosberry was right about one thing.

This season was proving to be a great deal more interesting than he'd expected.

CHAPTER
SEVEN

"Lord Melrose was in a good humor for a gentleman who's the talk of every gossip in London, wasn't he, my dears?"

"Perhaps he's in a good humor because he's escaped Lady Christine Dingley's clutches." Juliet's lips curved in a wicked grin. "That reminds me, my lady. I heard Lady Quigley whisper Lady Christine's name to you at the linen drapers. What has she got to do with it?"

"Oh, I nearly forgot! My dears, it's the most shocking thing! You won't believe it."

Emmeline said nothing, but she suspected she *would* believe it, every terrible word.

Juliet gave a bored shrug. "I can't imagine it could be anything too shocking. I've never seen a more perfect belle than Lady Christine. Did she stumble during the cotillion?"

"Or step on her partner's foot? Spill lemonade on her silk gown? Would that be enough to earn the lifelong ire of the *ton*?" Emmeline tried to smile, but under her forced gaiety, her chest had gone as tight as a noose. She'd made a dreadful mess of everything, and now her own lies were closing in on her like a snare around the neck of a helpless rabbit.

Lady Fosberry's eyes were wide. "All of London is clamoring to know the identity of the Lady in Lavender, as you know, and the *ton* had it that it was Lady Christine in the library with Lord Melrose, if you can credit it."

"Lady Christine!" Emmeline exclaimed. "I don't see what reason they have to suspect her. There must have been two dozen ladies wearing purple gowns last night."

"Not purple, dear, but *lavender*. You do recall that bit of silliness in *The Times* about Lady Christine squabbling with Lady Philippa over a length of lavender silk?"

Emmeline stared at Lady Fosberry, horrified. "Do you mean to say the *ton* would ruin a young lady's reputation over some absurd bit of gossip in *The Times*?"

"I'm afraid so. The *ton* doesn't care one whit about accuracy when it comes to their gossip."

"But it doesn't make any sense it would be Lady Christine," Juliet protested. "Why should she risk her reputation by trifling with a gentleman she's likely to become betrothed to in a matter of weeks?"

"*If* she can bring him up to scratch. She hasn't so far, you know, and it's only a few weeks until the end of the season. The worst of the gossips are saying Lady Christine will do whatever it takes to become the Countess of Melrose."

"Even *ruin* herself?" Juliet's face darkened. "I don't believe a word of it."

Emmeline pressed a hand to her forehead and squeezed her eyes closed, but there was no shutting it out, no pretending it wasn't happening. She had to tell Lady Fosberry the truth at once. She couldn't allow an innocent lady to take the blame for her own disgraceful conduct with Lord Melrose. "My lady," she began, her voice trembling. "I must tell you—"

"But you needn't worry about Lady Christine," Lady Fosberry went on. "Lord Cudworth overheard Lord Quigley gossiping about Lady Christine at White's—rascals, the lot of them—and declared it could not have been her, as he'd just been dancing with her, and had returned her to her father only moments before."

Emmeline released the breath she'd been holding, but her relief was short-lived. Lady Christine's narrow escape didn't solve her own predicament. If she didn't tell Juliet and Lady Fosberry the truth—if she didn't own up to her, er...how had Lord Cross put it? Her amorous encounter with Lord Melrose—the noose would strangle her.

But if she *did* tell them, she'd find herself the Countess of Melrose before the end of the season. No doubt every other young lady in London would be thrilled with such an outcome, but not Emmeline. A match between them went against every logical principle in the scientific realm.

And that was to say nothing of the human realm.

She couldn't imagine two people less suited to each other than she and Lord Melrose. It would be like pairing a sun- and heat-thirsty tea rose with a shade-loving climber, and expecting them to thrive in the same part of the garden.

"Whatever is the matter with Lord Melrose's friend, Lord Cross?" Juliet asked suddenly. "He never smiled once during their call this morning. He seems determined to be displeased with everyone and everything. It makes one wish to tease a grin out of him."

Lady Fosberry sighed. "Poor Cross is destined to die a lonely eccentric. He's dreadfully clever, you know, but so somber! None of the young ladies can please him, and they're all terrified of him."

Juliet, who was terrified of no one, let out a derisive snort. "Pity. I rather fancied a dance with him last night."

"Well, dearest, better Lord Cross than Lord Boggs." Lady Fosberry settled her skirts with an offended sniff.

Juliet smiled. "Ah, but Lord Cross never asked me, did he?"

"He never asked anyone, the blackguard, and you were right to scold him for it. But never mind Lord Boggs and Lord Cross. Gentlemen are tiresome creatures, are they not?" Lady Fosberry peered out the window as the carriage turned and made its way up the drive toward the house. "Now, Juliet, I advise you to retire to your bedchamber and rest this afternoon, before Lady Emory's ball this evening,"

"Yes, my lady," Juliet said, meekly enough.

The carriage came to a stop and the driver appeared at the door and handed Lady Fosberry out. Emmeline slid across the bench to follow her, but before she could accept the coachman's hand, Juliet wrapped her fingers around Emmeline's wrist. "A word, Emmeline?"

Emmeline fell back against the seat, her heart suddenly racing at the uncharacteristically serious expression on her sister's face.

Juliet waited until Lady Fosberry was out of sight

before she turned to Emmeline, then she paused, as if choosing her words carefully. Finally, she asked, "Is there something you wish to tell me, Emmeline?"

Something? There were a hundred things, each more worrying than the last. Emmeline's kiss with Lord Melrose, the unexpected emotions that had overwhelmed her since that kiss, the dozens of lies she'd told, and those she had yet to tell—lies that threatened to trap her as surely as a fly in a spider's web, as lies always did.

Emmeline's mouth opened, all of these confessions rushing to her lips, but only one word emerged. "No?"

Juliet gazed at her for a long time while Emmeline squirmed under that penetrating stare. "Are you quite sure?"

"Er...yes?"

"Because it occurs to me *you* were wearing a lavender gown the night of Lady Fosberry's—"

"No, I wasn't. It was *amethyst*."

"Amethyst," Juliet repeated flatly.

"Yes, and it wasn't a ball gown at all, but a day dress."

"I see. You happened to be wearing an amethyst dress on the same evening you mysteriously disappeared from our bedchamber, and Lord Melrose is said to have been cavorting with a young lady in a similar gown at that very same time, and when you returned you were flushed and breathless, and the two things having nothing to do with each other?"

Emmeline swallowed. "I wouldn't say cavorting, exactly—"

"Now Lord Melrose has just happened to come upon you at Floris, and invited you to visit Lady

Finchley's rose garden, all while he was staring at you the way Tilly stares at sugarplums? You'd have me believe all of this is merely a coincidence?"

Lord Melrose, staring at her? Surely not.

"I..." Emmeline began, then fell silent.

She longed to confide everything to Juliet—to lay her head on Juliet's shoulder and let the truth spill out of her until she'd exhausted herself, but she held her tongue, even as her throat ached with the effort to keep from blurting out the truth.

If Juliet discovered Emmeline was indeed the Lady in Lavender, it would be the death knell to any possibility of a marriage between Juliet and Lord Melrose, and Emmeline didn't intend to let that happen.

Emmeline and Phee had been wrong about Lord Melrose's pattern. He'd proven to be far more adventurous than either of them had anticipated, and Phee's original reasons for pairing him with Juliet were as sound as they'd ever been.

Emmeline may have managed to make a dreadful mess of things, but a few ill-advised kisses in a dark library didn't make Juliet and Lord Melrose any less suited to each other than they'd been before.

It wasn't just that Juliet was uncommonly pretty, and Lord Melrose uncommonly handsome. If matchmaking were simply a matter of pairing the handsomest gentleman with the prettiest lady, there'd be no challenge to it at all. After all, Lady Christine was a fair, delicate beauty, and she was still a poor match for Lord Melrose.

Phee liked to talk about patterns and number sequences, but matchmaking wasn't *just* about mathematics. It was human psychology as well, and statistics and philosophy. Even zoology was part of it, when one considered the ways in which human behavior mimicked animal behavior, and anthropology too, given the evolution of norms regarding mating and marriage as civilization advanced.

And of course, there was botany.

Matchmaking was no different than choosing an ideally matched pair of roses, and breeding or grafting them together to create a perfect bloom. Indeed, the two things were so remarkably alike, she wondered why everyone didn't see it, but then not many people saw things the way she did.

It was about character, temperament, intellect, instinct and...oh, very well, the fact that both Juliet and Lord Melrose were exceedingly beautiful didn't *hurt* matters. They were each perfect in their own way, but they'd be even more stunning together than they ever could be apart, just as a perfect hybrid was.

Still, there *was* one thing that concerned Emmeline about this endeavor, and that was that even attempting a match between them went against every conceivable scientific principle.

An immutable rule of experimentation was that the greatest risks yielded the greatest reward. The most adventurous scientist didn't shy away from a challenge—not if the reward was great enough—but the wisest among them were cautious with their research and attempted to achieve a balance between risk and reward in their experimentation.

There was no greater reward this season than Lord Melrose, and no greater risk than stealing the Nonesuch from the Incomparable in order to wed him to one of the infamous Templetons, especially with the Lady in Lavender scandal hanging over them like the sword of Damocles.

The trick would be in getting Juliet and Lord Melrose to fall in love with the least amount of risk possible.

There was no question of lying to Lord Melrose about the Lady in Lavender, or attempting to persuade him it had been Juliet he'd kissed in the library. Emmeline would *never* lie about such a thing, or try to trick a gentleman into marriage.

But she wouldn't need to lie to anyone. Juliet and Lord Melrose were predisposed to become enamored of each other. Once they did, everyone would forget all about this foolishness with the Lady in Lavender.

Really, when one looked at it scientifically, wasn't a match between Juliet and Lord Melrose simply setting things back in order, so they might progress as they were meant to from the start? It should have been Juliet in that library with him, not Emmeline. She was an anomaly, a mutation, a flaw in the experiment that should have been corrected before it could happen.

And it wasn't as if Lord Melrose had a particular longing for *her*. He'd cast her more than a passing glance at Floris, yes, but he still hadn't the vaguest idea she was the lady he'd kissed last night. He wasn't likely to ever figure it out, nor did Emmeline wish him to.

She wasn't destined to become a countess. She'd never flourish in the brightest patch of sunlight in the garden. She was meant to remain at Hambleden Manor, digging in the dirt for the rest of her days and breeding her father's roses.

She'd never minded being alone, but Juliet couldn't be happy with such a solitary existence. She must have people around her, a life filled with sound and color and romance. With every lonely day that passed at home, Juliet grew more despondent, her plans for the life she'd always dreamed of withering on the vine.

She deserved happiness far beyond what she could ever find at Hambleden Manor—far beyond what she could hope for from a marriage with Lord Boggs. If Juliet married Lord Melrose, she'd have all the society she could ever wish for, and a doting husband besides, and it would put a quick end to any possibility of a match between Juliet and Lord Boggs.

"Is that what you'd have me believe, Emmeline? That this is all a coincidence?"

Emmeline dragged her attention back to her sister. "I...yes, I suppose it must be."

Her cheeks heated with shame at the lie, and she had to look away from the disappointment in Juliet's eyes.

"Very well. If you change your mind and decide you *do* wish to tell me something, I'll be more than happy to hear it." Juliet reached for Emmeline's hand, squeezed it, and without another word, quietly withdrew.

Emmeline remained alone in the carriage for a long time after that, thinking. When she did rouse herself to go inside and passed the round gilt table in the entryway, she came to a stop. There, right in the center of the marble top sat an enormous spray of pink hothouse roses that had arrived while they were out.

She plucked up the card from the table.

They were for Juliet, from Lord Boggs, with a request that she save him her first two dances at Lady Emory's ball that night.

Juliet, and Lord Boggs.

No. It was out of the question. A marriage be-tween them would be as much of a disaster as a mar-riage between Emmeline and Lord Melrose.

The card fluttered from her fingers and fell to the floor. She slid it under the table leg with her foot, then turned and slowly mounted the stairs.

Tomorrow, they'd all visit Lady Finchley's rose garden, the ideal setting in which to nurture a fledg-ling romance. Emmeline would find the rose she needed to complete the perfume, and Juliet and Lord Melrose would discover they were meant for each other.

Everyone would get what they wanted.

For two people as perfectly matched as Juliet and Lord Melrose, falling in love would be the easiest thing in the world.

CHAPTER
EIGHT

The sky above was a glorious, celestial blue, the sun's rays were bright and warm upon the ground, and every breath they took was sweetened with the honeyed scent of Lady Finchley's roses.

Wasn't love meant to happen on just such a day, and in just such a place? Conditions were ideal for a budding romance to germinate and grow, but Emmeline had never seen two utterly irresistible people more determined to resist each other than Juliet and the Earl of Melrose.

They didn't appear at all interested in becoming besotted. Emmeline had held her breath every time Lord Melrose addressed Juliet, searching his face for any sign that he was already infatuated with her vivacious sister, but his expression revealed only polite, detached interest.

As for Juliet, if anything, she was worse than Lord Melrose. Oh, she was as charming and lively as ever, but she'd hardly spared Lord Melrose a glance, instead reserving her most dazzling smiles and sparkling conversation for Lord Cross, who seemed not to have the vaguest notion what to do with them, or her.

Juliet hadn't even noticed the way Lord Melrose's smart navy coat made his eyes look so impossibly blue, Emmeline wished it were possible to breed blue roses, so she might create one just that same shade of cornflower.

Blue roses, of all absurd things. They didn't even *exist* in nature.

None of this made any sense. Why couldn't they just get on with falling in love, so Emmeline could return to the safety of her own walled garden at Hambleden Manor?

The fault must lie with her. She was doing something wrong—

"Will you join me in a stroll under the rose arbors, Miss Templeton? If you're not too fatigued, that is."

Emmeline looked up into Lord Melrose's warm blue eyes, then turned a longing gaze on the closely planted row of arbors, each so thick with blossoms it was like walking through a magical passageway made entirely of roses.

She *would* like to join him—that is, not him, precisely. It had nothing to do with *him*.

She was merely eager to go on a search for the elusive damask rose she needed to recreate her father's perfume, and couldn't think of a better place to search than under arches dripping with roses.

But it would be far better for him to have a romantic stroll in the gardens with Juliet. "I'm rather fatigued, my lord, but perhaps my sister would care for a—"

"I daresay a stroll won't tax your strength terribly much, Emmeline," Juliet called from behind them, where she'd paused beside a stone bench with Lord Cross and Lady Fosberry. "You've been going on for months about including rose arches in the garden at Hambleden Manor."

Emmeline cast a sidelong glance at Lord Melrose, but his handsome face showed only tepid curiosity, and not the rapacious glee with which the *ton* received any mention of the Templetons, even one so innocent as rose arbors in the manor garden. "Well, I don't—"

"Such spectacular roses! I can't bear for you to miss anything, Emmeline. Perhaps Lord Melrose would be kind enough to take you to visit the damask roses afterwards." Juliet gave them both a bright smile. "I'm certain you'll discover dozens of clusters to mash together."

"Species, not clusters," Emmeline corrected. "And the proper term is graft, not—"

"Yes, do go on, Emmeline." Lady Fosberry settled herself on the bench and arranged her parasol to shade her face from the sun. "You can tell us all about the canes and rosehips and crowns and things when you return."

"Shall we, Miss Templeton?" Lord Melrose smiled down at her, the breeze fingering his hair, and there was little Emmeline could do but take his arm.

"I wasn't aware roses wore crowns," Lord Melrose murmured as he led her down a tidy pathway lined on each side by a purple blaze of lavender. "I feel as if I've been misled, somehow."

Emmeline couldn't help but laugh, though a part of her resented it. This would be a great deal easier if he'd stop being so agreeable. "The crown is the point where the submerged roots meet the emerging canes."

It was, according to some botanists, the essence of the rose's vitality, the beating heart of the plant, but the idea of speaking of vitality to a gentleman made her cheeks warm.

"Ah, I see." He was quiet for a moment as they wandered down the pathways between the over-flowing flower beds, then, "I don't believe you've been perfectly honest with me, Miss Templeton."

Emmeline's steps faltered. "I, ah...I don't under-stand, my lord."

Had he realized she was the lady he'd kissed in Lady Fosberry's library? Or had he known all along, and lured her into the privacy of Lady Finchley's rose arbors to confront her? Her fingers tightened on his coat sleeve as a wave of emotion she couldn't identify rolled over her.

Anticipation, or dread. Goodness, when did one ever feel so much like the other? She'd certainly never noticed it before.

What could she possibly say in reply, if he did question her? She hadn't said a word throughout their entire encounter in the library, not even when he'd kissed her neck. She hadn't demanded he stop, or even pulled away from him. No, she'd arched back against him, as if begging him to keep going.

How could she possibly explain such a—

"Yesterday at Floris you claimed only a cursory knowledge of scent, but I don't think that's the truth." He turned his face down to hers, the dappled sunlight catching his golden eyelashes. "I think you're a great deal more knowledgeable than you claim."

Oh. Well, of course. What had she thought he meant?

"Confess it, Miss Templeton. Weren't you attempting to charm the perfumer's deepest secrets from Mr. Beale?"

Charm? No one had ever accused her of being charming before. "You're quite right. You've, ah... you've caught me out, my lord."

Emmeline smiled, but her cheeks heated with a strange combination of disappointment and relief, and inexplicably, with shame, as if his inability to recognize her was *her* fault.

Which was perfectly absurd, given she'd already made up her mind it was imperative he *not* recognize her, as it would ruin all her careful plans. Juliet and Lord Melrose must marry, and she intended to see the thing done as quickly as possible, and done sensibly, using the solid *scientific* principles of botany.

A grafting was what was needed here. The cultivar of one rose is inserted into the rootstock of another to create the scion, which the botanist then nurtures with water, rich soil, plenty of warm sunshine, and careful tending until the fuse between them takes, and a delicate new hybrid is born.

Lady Fosberry might tease her about her scientific approach to making matches, but Emmeline never used tools she didn't understand, and she understood *this*. Grafting roses was a clean, simple, predictable process, and one with a statistical chance of success.

But there could be no further scandal, no unpleasant surprises, and no losing her wits over Lord Melrose. No matter how handsome he was, or how soft his lips, or—

"Your interest in flowers isn't merely a hobby, either," Lord Melrose went on. "It's much more than that. You're a botanist, aren't you?"

A warm rush of pleasure flooded Emmeline's chest at his words. No one had ever called her a botanist before. Unless he meant it sarcastically? She glanced up at him, but he was smiling down at her, his handsome face alight with interest. "A novice botanist, I suppose."

"You follow in your father's learned footsteps, then?"

Emmeline's eyes widened. The *ton* seemed to have forgotten all about James Templeton after her mother's scandal and his retreat from society. Aside from Lady Fosberry, even those who'd once been his friends had abandoned him. No one had dared mention either of her parents to her since then, though she knew the *ton* spoke of the Templetons readily enough behind their backs.

"You know of my father's work?" she asked cautiously.

Lord Melrose looked surprised. "Yes, of course. James Templeton is quite well known in Royal Society circles."

"He, ah...yes. He was a scientist, mainly a chemist and a botanist. He created his own hybrid rose garden at our home in Buckinghamshire." It had been so long since Emmeline had discussed her father with anyone but her sisters or Lady Fosberry the words came slowly, awkward and creaky on her lips. "I didn't like to see his garden go to ruin after he died, so I took up where he left off."

Her father had encouraged hers and her sisters' natural curiosity. He'd been a brilliant man, and had taught them sciences, mathematics, literature, and languages, much to their mother's outrage.

A spinster in the making, her nose forever thrust between the pages of a book. No gentleman wants a bluestocking for a wife.

Emmeline's lack of prospects was the reason their mother had insisted she and Phee share their first season. She'd announced she wouldn't be put to the trouble of bringing out a girl who hadn't a prayer of catching a husband.

As it happened, Alice Templeton had been proved right. Neither Emmeline nor Phee had had a prayer of making a decent match, but not for the reasons their mother had supposed.

"Does your estate in Buckinghamshire have extensive grounds, Miss Templeton?"

Emmeline managed to smother her very unladylike snort at the word 'estate,' and shook her head. "No, both the house and the grounds are quite small, but it's...it's home."

"I understand. I prefer the country to London." Lord Melrose glanced up at the sky, his blue eyes narrowing against the flood of sunlight on his face. "It's unfashionable of me, but I find the city begins to press in on me over time."

"Your younger sisters don't spend much time in London, I believe?" Emmeline ventured, after a silence. Lord Melrose was said to be utterly devoted to his sisters, and Emmeline, who treasured her own sisters, was curious to hear how he'd speak of them.

"Not much, no. It's my opinion that they're too young for London, though my eldest sister Margaret does not happen to share that opinion."

His lips curved in a rueful smile that lured an answering smile from Emmeline's lips.

"Henrietta and Sarah, my two younger sisters adore the country, but Margaret finds it terribly dull." His brows drew together as if he were baffled by the vicissitudes of a young lady's mind. He was such a picture of the doting but puzzled elder brother, a trill of sudden laughter escaped Emmeline.

He jerked towards her as if surprised, a quick grin rising to his lips. "You have a lovely laugh, Miss Templeton. Has anyone ever told you that?"

No one but Emmeline's father and sisters had ever told her she had a lovely *anything*. That same rush of warmth suffused her, tingling through her veins until she fairly vibrated with pleasure. She raised her eyes to his, he met her gaze, and for the time it took for Emmeline's heart to beat once... twice...a third time...neither of them looked away.

At last, Lord Melrose dropped his gaze, and as soon as those lovely cornflower blue eyes released her from their thrall, Emmeline recalled with a pang that she wasn't *meant* to be drowning in Lord Melrose's eyes.

But they were well into the rose arbors by now, the blooms surrounding them heavy with fragrance, and so thick Emmeline could no longer see the entrance behind them, or the exit ahead. It was as if Juliet, Lord Cross, and Lady Fosberry had vanished, leaving her alone in a cocoon of silken petals with Lord Melrose.

"There's a bench, just there." He nodded to a low stone bench nestled under an arch smothered with pale, creamy roses that released a refreshing scent of wintergreen. "Shall we rest for a while?"

Emmeline knew she should refuse. That she should take him back to Juliet, and attempt to manage it so he and her sister were seated beside each other in the carriage for the ride back to Hampstead Heath.

But that wasn't what she did.

She *meant* to. Indeed, she opened her mouth to do just that, but somehow, she found she couldn't push the refusal past her lips.

It was one afternoon only, and she *did* so want to see the roses.

~

"I'D WATCH my back if I were you, Melrose. Lady Christine doesn't carry a muff pistol, does she?"

Johnathan was sprawled in front of the fire in his study, staring down at the last swallow of port in his tumbler, his mind on...nothing whatsoever, but he roused himself at Cross's words.

"Lady Christine?" Good Lord, he'd nearly forgotten about her. Odd, that he could so easily forget about the lady he'd been resigned to marrying at the start of the season. "What's the matter with her? It's not the silver hairbrush again, is it?"

Cross peered over the top of his paper, one dark eyebrow aloft. "You can't be that obtuse, Melrose. She's furious that..." He glanced back at the paper. "'A shameless seductress in a lavender gown' has upended her betrothal, and ruined all her happiness.'"

Good Lord, would the fuss over a betrothal that never existed ever end? He hadn't once shown a partiality for Lady Christine, much less asked her to marry him. "Lady Christine and I were never betrothed."

"No, but all of London expected you would be, and among them Lady Dingley, who declares her daughter is..." Cross read aloud from the paper again. "'So humiliated she can't ever show her face in society again.'"

Johnathan rolled his eyes. "I don't know what she's on about. Lord Cudworth is Lady Christine's for the plucking."

"Ah, but Lord Cudworth isn't the Nonesuch, and is, at least according to the papers, a poor replacement for him."

"This is all according to the papers, is it?" Johnathan let out a derisive snort. "It's nonsense, Cross. *The Times* claims Lady Christine attended Lord Lambeth's ball just last night, and danced every dance. They went on at tedious length about her gown, too."

Cross tossed the paper aside. "Lady Dingley vows revenge, Melrose."

"That's absurd. Revenge against whom?"

"Against the shameless seductress in the lavender gown, of course," Cross said with a sigh, as if Johnathan were trying his patience.

"What makes Lady Christine think she'll ever find out the identity of the lady? I haven't, and I'm the one who kissed her." It had been two days, and Johnathan still couldn't be certain which sister—Emmeline, or Juliet Templeton—was the Lady in Lavender.

Of the two of them, Juliet Templeton made the most sense. She was bolder than her sister, and she'd been in the ballroom that evening dressed in some shade of purple silk. A shade darker than lavender, yes, but one couldn't trust Cudworth to know the difference.

Yes, rationally speaking, Juliet Templeton was the obvious choice, but there was something about Emmeline Templeton...

He couldn't resist her shy smile, that adorable blush and her lovely, smoky blue eyes. Her cleverness, her earnestness, her lack of artifice puzzled, intrigued, and charmed him all at once.

Of the two sisters, Emmeline was the one who made his heart quicken in his chest, but he couldn't be certain it was she, and not her sister who was the Lady in Lavender. It would hardly endear him to either one of them to admit it though, or God forbid, if he should offer for one and it turned out to be the other—

"A lady scorned has resources beyond what you could ever imagine, Melrose."

"Oh?" Johnathan forced his attention back to Cross, who was still going on about Lady Dingley. "What resources are those?"

"The most diabolical resources of all, namely, the other ladies in London, all of whom profess themselves highly offended by the Lady in Lavender."

"Let them be offended, then. I don't see what business it is of theirs."

"The gossips make everything their business, Melrose. They've come up with a list between them, with the name of every chit at Lady Fosberry's ball who was wearing any shade of purple you can possibly imagine."

"A list of young ladies in lavender won't do them much good, Cross, unless they can pinpoint which of them was the one seen leaving the library."

"They've gotten a description of her gown from Lord Cudworth, and they intend to take it to Madame Toussaint, who supplied gowns to nearly every young lady in London this season, and find her out that way."

"Lord Cudworth doesn't know a damn thing about gowns," Johnathan muttered, but an uneasy feeling was gnawing at him.

It wasn't a bad idea, all told. He turned his gaze back to fire, mulling over this new information. Yes, it was a good idea—rather *too* good. They'd find out the lady's identity soon enough, and she'd be flayed open on the dagger's edge of every vicious tongue in London.

Unless he found her first.

If he and his mystery lady weren't already betrothed by the time the gossips discovered who she was, there was every chance they'd drive her from London with their venom, in just the same way the Templeton sisters had been driven out, clutching the shreds of their ruined reputations around them like tattered clothing.

Emmeline Templeton's face flashed in his mind then, the shy curve of her lips, and the husky laugh that had so surprised him this afternoon. He didn't like to think of how that smile must have dimmed when, through no fault of their own, the Templeton sisters had landed on the wrong side of the *ton*.

"You didn't seem to have much to say during our outing today," Johnathan said, determined to change the subject.

"When have you ever known me to be loquacious, Melrose?"

"Never." Cross wasn't one for polite chitchat, but he'd been unusually quiet today.

"I didn't speak much because Juliet Templeton didn't cease talking long enough for me to get a word in. I've never seen a woman with a more wearisome tongue."

"But such a pretty face." Johnathan shot a sly look at Cross.

"I didn't notice."

"Of *course* you bloody did! You're a man, aren't you? I don't know why you bother to deny it, Cross. It's perfectly acceptable to admire a lady without becoming betrothed to her."

"God forbid I ever become betrothed to Juliet Templeton. I'd never have another moment's peace."

"You could do with less peace. You haven't got nearly enough to plague you. It's not good for a man to get his own way too often."

Cross rolled his eyes. "This, from *you*? I'd say you get your way often enough, Melrose."

"Not a bit of it. Have you forgotten I have three sisters?"

Cross chuckled, and they both fell into a silence made comfortable by a long friendship, each lost in their own musings, until Johnathan disrupted the moment of peace. "I'm going to marry her, Cross. The Lady in Lavender. I'm going to marry her."

He'd made up his mind to it the same night he'd kissed her, mere moments after she'd fled, and left him alone in the library, her scent still wrapped around him.

Cross sighed, but he didn't seem surprised. "Yes, I suppose you don't have much choice."

No, he didn't—not unless he wished to be condemned as a rake and a scoundrel—but that wasn't the reason Johnathan was so determined to make the Lady in Lavender his countess.

He turned the tumbler in his hand, gazing at the play of firelight over the last swallow of rich, dark-red port, glittering like a ruby through the thick crystal. The night of Lady Fosberry's ball, when he'd been so deep in his cups, he'd thought his uncharacteristic drunkenness a minor rebellion.

In truth, it had been the first in a series of unexpected moments that had altered the entire course of his life, like the first drops of rain preceding a storm that swept all before it, and left everything in its wake forever changed.

Had he not been in his cups, he never would have chased after Lady Susanna, and ended up kissing the Lady in Lavender.

It was strange, the way a man's entire life could change in the space of a single evening, but wasn't the mere fact of it having happened evidence that he and the Lady in Lavender were destined for each other? Surely, fate wouldn't have allowed such an extraordinary chain of circumstances to unfold otherwise?

Johnathan had never thought of himself as a romantic, but perhaps no man ever did until the fates smiled on him, and threw him into the path of the one woman who tipped his world on its axis. That he didn't know her name, and hadn't even seen her face, made not the slightest difference at all.

"I only hope the Lady in Lavender will make a proper Countess of Melrose. You have your sisters to think of."

"There's never a time when I *don't* think of them, Cross."

"I know." Cross tossed back the rest of his port. "What's your opinion of Emmeline Templeton? She's a quiet young lady, unlike her sister, but she seemed happy enough to talk to you today."

"She's..." Johnathan paused, uncertain how to put into words what Emmeline Templeton was. Nothing like any other lady he'd ever known, and not as he'd imagined any lady ever could be, before their visit to Lady Fosberry's drawing room yesterday.

He was still missing a great many of the pieces that made up the puzzle of Emmeline Templeton, but the more time he spent with her, the more determined he was to find them.

Those eyes, and that guilty flush...

"Unexpected." It wasn't quite the right word, but it was the best Johnathan could do. "She's unexpected."

It wasn't until he'd retired to his bedchamber that night, and was staring up at the canopy over his head that Johnathan realized he'd spent hardly any time talking to Juliet Templeton.

He'd meant to do so in hopes of solving the mystery of which Templeton sister was the Lady in Lavender, but somehow, he'd forgotten all about it.

CHAPTER
NINE

"My dears, the *ton* has gone mad."

Emmeline inserted her thumb between the pages of the book she'd been pretending to read—poor Mr. Whateley again—and turned from her place on the window seat, where she'd been daydreaming for the better part of an hour. Somehow, Mr. Whateley's observations on convex and concave shapes of ground couldn't quite hold her attention.

Juliet, who'd been staring as vacantly at the fire as Emmeline had been at the window, turned with a dismayed sigh. "Oh, no. What is it *this* time?"

"Why, only listen. Lord Batty grievously insulted Miss Goswick at his ball last night by inviting her to accompany him to his library!" Lady Fosberry lowered *The Morning Gazette*, her eyes wide over the top of the page. "It seems he was convinced *she* is the Lady in Lavender, and therefore was already ruined!"

Lady Fosberry tossed *The Gazette* aside and snatched up *The Times*, tutting as she scanned the page. "Well, how ridiculous! As if the *ton* weren't in enough of an uproar, Lord Cudworth now claims the gown the Lady in Lavender was wearing wasn't *lavender* at all, but..."

Emmeline's heart quickened as Lady Fosberry squinted down at the gossip section of the paper. She'd kept well out of sight at Lady Fosberry's ball, but if it got about that the gown wasn't a gown at all, and wasn't lavender, but amethyst—

"Periwinkle. *Periwinkle!*" Lady Fosberry threw her hands up in the air in disgust. "Periwinkle and lavender aren't a thing alike! Lord Cudworth is a very great fool, to be sure."

"May I see it?" Juliet rose from the settee and plopped down beside Lady Fosberry, who handed over the paper. "Do you suppose he's in love with the Lady in Lavender after a single encounter? It would be excessively romantic if he were."

"If he was in love with her, wouldn't he know her the moment he saw her again?"

The bitter edge to Emmeline's voice made Juliet's brows rise.

Dash it. Why couldn't she keep her mouth closed?

"If he *has* seen her again, that is." Emmeline swallowed. "I have no way of knowing if he has or not, of course, or anything else about it, really."

Lady Fosberry frowned. "How should you, dearest?"

"The scandal is far too delicious for the *ton* to let it go now." Juliet folded the paper and set it aside. "The only way to prevent a truly ugly outcome is for the Lady in Lavender to become betrothed to Lord Melrose before her identity is discovered."

"Of course you're right, my dear. Honestly, I don't understand why the lady hasn't made her identity known." Lady Fosberry wrung her hands. "I don't like to see a young lady ruined. Why do you suppose her family hasn't come forward?"

"Perhaps they don't know. She may not have told her family about her predicament." Emmeline tossed Mr. Whateley aside with more force than necessary. "Perhaps she hasn't told anyone at all, or else she did, and the family fled London for the country with plans to return next season, once the scandal dies down."

Lady Fosberry shook her head. "But surely anyone who knows Lord Melrose realizes he'll do what is expected of any honorable gentleman who impugns a lady's reputation."

"Whether he's in love with her or not, it's clear he intends to marry her." Juliet's gaze was fixed on Emmeline. "If the Lady in Lavender were wise, she'd make herself known at once."

"Make herself known, and marry a gentleman who doesn't love her? A gentleman she trapped into marriage—whether inadvertently or not—who will likely resent her for it?"

Emmeline couldn't say when *love*, of all things, had become so vitally important to a marriage when only weeks ago she would have said one thing hadn't anything to do with the other.

Somehow, all that had changed.

"But of *course* she must marry him, dearest." Lady Fosberry spoke as if it were perfectly obvious, and she wished the matter settled.

"Well, it strikes me as odd that the Lady in Lavender hasn't come forward by now." Juliet hadn't taken her eyes off Emmeline. "It's been three days! I tell you, there's something strange about this business, my lady. What do *you* make of it, Emmeline?"

"I, ah...I hardly know. I'm at as much of a loss as

you both are." Emmeline didn't dare look at her sister, but she could feel Juliet's gaze still boring into her, so intense it was a wonder her hair didn't burst into flames.

"Well, I can't help but admire the Lady in Lavender, though an amorous encounter with Lord Melrose in the middle of a ball was a remarkably foolish thing to do. *Remarkably* foolish. Don't you think it was a *remarkably foolish* thing to do, Emmeline?"

Emmeline squirmed in her seat. "Er, as to that, I daresay it wasn't—"

"I begin to think you were right, Lady Fosberry, about the unpredictable nature of people. Why, the most unexpected events might yet occur before the season's over. Don't you agree about the unexpected events, Emmeline?"

The look Juliet gave Emmeline sent a rush of heat into Emmeline's cheeks, and she slumped down in her seat, wishing Lady Fosberry's plump window cushions would devour her.

"Still, I can't imagine what could have come over the Lady in Lavender. She's either very brave, or very foolish. Emmeline, can *you* imagine what might have come over the Lady in Lavender?"

"No. How should I?" Emmeline turned back toward the window to avoid the knowing look in Juliet's eyes.

"Do stop teasing your sister, Juliet. She looks a trifle peaked. Are you quite all right, dear?"

"Just a slight headache, my lady," Emmeline muttered, squeezing her eyes closed.

"I daresay you've had too much sun this morning. Come away from the window, child." Lady Fosberry patted the seat beside her on the settee. "For my part,

I think the Lady in Lavender need not despair entirely of a love match. There's a desperation to Lord Melrose's search for her that hints at something more than duty. I think he cares for the lady, and that's why—"

"I beg your pardon, my lady." Watkins, Lady Fosberry's butler, came into the drawing room. "Lady Dingley and Lady Christine are here, and they're quite anxious to speak to you."

Lady Fosberry's eyes shot into her hairline. "Are they, indeed? Well, by all means, Watkins, show them in. My goodness," Lady Fosberry whispered after Watkins left the room. "What do you suppose *they* want?"

Juliet rolled her eyes. "I don't dare speculate."

A moment later Lady Dingley and Lady Christine swept into the drawing room and crowded onto the settee across from Lady Fosberry, neither of them offering so much as a nod to either Emmeline or Juliet. They may as well not have been in the room, for all the notice Lady Dingley and her daughter took of them.

Lady Fosberry frowned, but she greeted Lady Dingley with forced cordiality. "My dear Lady Dingley, how do you do?"

"Why, we're perfectly awful, Lady Fosberry! My palpitations are so dreadful I could hardly drag myself out of bed this morning, and only look at my poor, dear Christine! Lord Melrose has broken her heart. He's a scoundrel, make no mistake."

If Lady Christine had looked the least bit heartbroken, Emmeline would have felt quite guilty, indeed, but there was no sorrow in those pretty blue eyes, no grief in the sullen pinch of her rosebud lips.

Lady Christine wasn't heartbroken. She was *furious*.

"Naturally, we came directly to you, my lady. I daresay I shouldn't be abroad at all in my sad condition, but I told Christine we simply must come to see you. 'Christine,' I said to her this morning, 'We must go and see Lady Fosberry.' The *ton* is laughing at us, but I knew *you* would never abandon us in our hour of need."

Lady Fosberry blinked, taken aback by this sudden display of tender affection from Lady Dingley. "Er, yes, of course. I'm happy to help, Lady Dingley, only I don't know what I can do."

"Why, you can tell me the name of every young lady who attended your ball the other night," Lady Dingley exclaimed, as if it were all perfectly obvious.

"I beg your pardon," Lady Fosberry said coolly. "But I don't see how that will improve matters."

"You don't suppose we're going to allow this so-called Lady in Lavender, or Lady in Periwinkle, or whatever godforsaken color Cudworth has decided upon today to destroy my poor Christine's happiness, do you? We mean to see her brought to account! Christine would be the Countess of Melrose by now if it weren't for that harlot!"

Emmeline gasped, appalled. Lord Cross had warned them it would come to this, but to hear such venom spewing directly from Lady Dingley's lips was distressing, indeed.

"Forgive me, Lady Dingley, but Lord Melrose has had the entire season to offer for your daughter. If he intended to do so, surely he'd have done it by now." Juliet appeared calm, but Emmeline recognized the flush on her sister's cheeks for the fury it was.

Lady Christine didn't deign to reply, but her cold blue gaze shot to Juliet's face, her eyes narrowing to slits.

"I'm afraid it's out of the question, Lady Dingley." Lady Fosberry's had gone from cool to icy.

Lady Dingley had been dabbing a lace-edged handkerchief to her eyes, but her tears dried on her cheeks in a burst of hot anger at Lady Fosberry's refusal. "I can't imagine what reason you'd have to refuse us, unless..."

For the first time since she'd sailed through the door, Lady Dingley seemed to become aware that Emmeline and Juliet were in the room. Her livid gaze went from one to the other of them, then back again. "Unless you already know the lady's name, and wish to keep it a secret?"

Lady Fosberry's face went so red Emmeline actually leapt to her feet. "My lady—"

"I beg your pardon, Lady Fosberry." Watkins entered, his face remaining as blank as any well-trained servant's did when he came upon his mistress in a towering fury. "Lord Melrose and Lord Cross are here."

Everyone in Lady Fosberry's drawing room froze with their faces turned toward the door in a freakish tableau that might have made Emmeline laugh, if she hadn't been on the verge of casting up her accounts.

Neither Lord Melrose nor Lord Cross were as circumspect as Watkins. Both gentlemen were smiling when they entered the room, but their smiles vanished the moment they caught sight of Lady Dingley and Lady Christine.

No one said anything for some moments, but then Lady Dingley fixed a watery blue eye on Lord

Melrose, and drew herself up with all the offended dignity of a lady who thought herself deeply wronged. "How wonderful to see you looking so very hale and hearty, Lord Melrose. If only I could say the same for my poor, dear Christine."

If Lady Dingley expected Lord Melrose to display any consciousness of guilt, she was disappointed. He merely offered Lady Christine a perfunctory bow. "I'm sorry to hear Lady Christine is unwell, madam."

"Well, I don't see how she could be otherwise, my lord, given the mortifying incidents of the past few days."

Lord Melrose raised an eyebrow at this, but otherwise his face remained blank. "Mortifying, my lady? I don't see how."

"Do you not?" Lady Dingley let out a shrill laugh. "My dear Lord Melrose, there has always been an understanding between our families—"

"Forgive me, madam, but there is no understanding beyond a hope expressed by my mother when I was no more than a child. I have never offered for Lady Christine. We are not now, nor have we ever been betrothed."

A shocked silence followed this bald statement. Lady Dingley was speechless, but her cheeks flushed an ominous red.

As for Lady Christine, she hadn't ventured a single word since she entered Lady Fosberry's drawing room, nor did she venture one now, but sat as silent as a cipher, her icy gaze moving between Lord Melrose and Juliet. At one point that glacial gaze fell on Emmeline, but just as quickly dismissed her.

"As the day is so fine, I thought perhaps Lord Cross and I might persuade you and your guests to accompany us on a drive to Greenwich, to see Lady Hammond's roses." Lord Melrose turned to Lady Fosberry with a bow.

Lady Dingley was growing ever more infuriated with every word out of Lord Melrose's mouth, but she didn't quite dare to challenge either him or Lady Fosberry any further, as both of them wielded considerable power with the *ton*.

So, instead she set her sights on the only two people in the room she imagined she could bully with impunity. "How kind you are, Lord Melrose, to show such an interest in the, ah...Misses Templeton."

Emmeline stiffened at the derisive note in Lady Dingley's voice when she spoke their name, but Juliet made a noise that sounded suspiciously like a smothered laugh.

Lord Cross's gaze darted to her, and the corners of his lips twitched, but Lord Melrose stiffened, his face going as hard as stone. "The pleasure is mine, Lady Dingley. They're both charming young ladies."

"Charming, yes. I believe their mother was thought charming, as well." Lady Christine said, breaking her icy silence at last, her voice dripping with sweetness even as she shot Juliet a poisonous smirk.

Emmeline went still at Lady Christine's taunt, all the louder and uglier for the moment of dead silence that followed it.

Had she misheard? Surely, she must have misunderstood...

But no, of course, she hadn't. In the time it took for her to release one breath and draw the next, she became painfully aware she hadn't misunderstood at all. If nothing else, she would have known it by the vicious triumph on Lady Christine's pretty face.

"Is there something you wish to say, Lady Christine?" Lady Fosberry looked as if she'd happily box Lady Christine's ears, but before two of London's most elegant ladies could fall into fisticuffs, Lord Melrose stepped into the fray.

And his *expression*...

Emmeline had never seen a gentleman more infuriated in her entire life. In the blink of an eye, his easy smile vanished, and his handsome face flushed with outrage. He stared at Lady Christine for a long, tense moment, every inch the haughty earl, then said in a low, hard voice, "I see I've made a narrow escape, my lady."

He said no more. There was no need. All the color drained from Lady Christine's face as she absorbed the full force of his meaning.

"Come, Christine. We have no friends *here*." Lady Dingley gathered the tarnished remnants of her dignity around herself, and marched from the room without another word, her daughter in her wake.

Emmeline waited until they'd left the room before sagging against the settee, fearful her legs would buckle beneath her. "Dear God, what a dreadful scene."

"How *dare* Lady Dingley and that perfectly awful daughter of hers presume to speak thus to me and my friends in my *own drawing room*?" Lady Fosberry's eyes were blazing. "Vicious chit!"

She went on for some time, railing against the Dingleys and declaring she'd never liked them, until at last she noticed neither Emmeline nor Juliet had said a word. "Now my dears, you mustn't take any-

NOT JUST ANY EARL

thing those two vindictive females say to heart. They represent the very worst of the *ton*. I know neither of you cares a fig for anything they have to say."

Juliet cleared her throat. "Of course not, my lady."

Emmeline must have risen to her feet at some point, though she couldn't recall when, because she was standing, her fingers gripping the back of the settee, her gaze fixed on Lord Melrose.

He took a step toward her, his face pale. "Emmeline?"

Emmeline said nothing. She couldn't speak.

No one, aside from Lady Fosberry, had *ever* spoken up in her family's defense. Not the day of the scandal, or any day in the three years since.

Until now.

Tears pressed behind her eyes. She held them ruthlessly at bay, shaking with the effort, but her expression must have revealed her distress, because Lord Melrose turned hastily to Lady Fosberry with a polite bow. "It occurs to me you all may be fatigued by our drive yesterday, my lady. Perhaps we should put off our visit to Greenwich until tomorrow. What say you, Cross?"

Lord Cross was gazing at Juliet, looking more uncertain than Emmeline had ever seen him. "Yes, of course, if the ladies prefer it."

"For my part, a drive sounds lovely. It's a beautiful day, and I won't let Lady Dingley spoil my pleasure in it." Juliet gave a defiant toss of her head.

Lady Fosberry regarded Emmeline in silence for a moment, then shook her head. "I think we'd all do better to rest this afternoon, as Lord Melrose suggests. Especially you, Emmeline. Go on up to your bedchamber, my dear. You look pale."

"Yes, my lady." Emmeline risked one last glance at Lord Melrose before leaving the drawing room, but she didn't return to her bedchamber. Instead, she slipped out the door and into the rose garden.

Thankfully, it was deserted.

Lady Fosberry's gardener had come in this morning and pruned the spent blooms from the rose canes, snipping them just above the foliage so the plant might produce more blossoms. He'd left an orderly row of thriving roses in his wake, the canes standing tall, each one aligned in perfect symmetry with those before and behind it, like soldiers on the march.

If only people would fall into tidy rows as prettily as roses did, but instead of the neat, logical conclusion Emmeline had hoped for, this business only grew more tangled. Not only had Lord Melrose *not* forgotten the Lady in Lavender as she'd predicted he would, he was also proving to be dreadfully stubborn about falling in love with Juliet.

Emmeline couldn't understand it. She'd been so certain putting the two of them together would be the simplest thing in the world, but somehow it wasn't working out as she'd thought it would.

She wandered toward the stone wall at the back of the garden, her feet silent against the soft ground. Lady Fosberry had warned her—she'd tried to make Emmeline understand people weren't logical or predictable, that emotions were slippery, and it was folly to think one could control them. Emmeline hadn't wanted to listen, but every day that passed was proving Lady Fosberry had been right all along.

Because ever since she'd kissed Lord Melrose, she hadn't recognized herself.

She reached out to stoke the glossy green leaves of a fragrant yellow rose at the end of the row closest to her, but the glide of the silky petals under her fingertips didn't soothe her as it usually did, so she knelt down, heedless of the dirt, and stuck her fingers a few inches into the soil at the base of the plant.

"This isn't resting in your bedchamber, Miss Templeton."

Emmeline's hands stilled for an instant, her breath catching in her throat, but she didn't turn around. "No, it's not. I'm afraid you've caught me, my lord."

"I've never known another lady who loves dirt the way you do."

From another man's lips the words might have been a taunt, but from his they were gentle and teasing, almost...*affectionate*.

He crouched next to her, watching the movement of her hands. "Will you tell me a little about what you're doing?"

Emmeline cast a shy glance up at him, then looked quickly away again when she realized how close he was. "Just making certain the soil is still damp. It dries quickly on warm, sunny days like today."

"Ah, I see. And here I thought you just enjoyed digging."

Emmeline smiled. "Well, I do."

His answering chuckle was soft and warm, like a summer breeze drifting over her skin. "What will you do next?"

No one had ever asked such a thing of Emmeline before—certainly not a handsome earl—but when she leaned back on her heels to see if he was making fun of her, she saw by the tender smile hovering at the corners of his lips that he wasn't.

Not at all.

She cleared the sudden lump from her throat, and tried to return his sweet smile. "Lady Fosberry's gardener takes excellent care of the roses, so there isn't much for me to do, but if this were my own garden in Buckinghamshire, I might walk down the rows to see which have bloomed, and check the leaves for signs of disease."

Lord Melrose got to his feet, and held out a hand to her. "Shall we do that, then?"

Emmeline looked up at him, at his handsome face cast in shadows, the sunlight behind him turning his hair a fiery gold, his hand held out to her, and something shifted inside her chest.

It wasn't painful, but it felt...final, as if it would never shift back again.

She accepted his hand, and they strolled down the rows together, Emmeline explaining how to remove diseased leaves from a plant as they went, and describing how to stake a rose so it might resist buffeting by the wind.

He listened, his head bent towards hers, and soon enough her reserve melted away, until she forgot herself and spoke to him as if he weren't the Earl of Melrose, or the Corinthian, or the Nonesuch, but as she might speak to a friend.

A very handsome friend, with kind eyes, and a devastating smile—

"Thank you for humoring me, Miss Templeton," he said, when they'd circled back to where they'd started.

Emmeline had opened her mouth to tell him

she'd enjoyed their stroll when he did something that made her words flutter away like petals scattering in the wind.

He raised her hand to his mouth, his gaze holding hers as he brushed his warm lips against her knuckles. There was nothing scandalous or improper in it, but Emmeline felt the brief, warm press of his lips deep in her belly, a seductive echo of his mouth gliding across her skin when he'd kissed her neck in the library.

"You won't forget our ride to Greenwich tomorrow, to see Lady Hammond's gardens?" He was still holding her hand, and the low, husky timber of his voice pulled another thrilling pulse from deep inside Emmeline's belly.

She swallowed. "I won't forget, my lord."

"Until tomorrow, then." He gave her fingertips a gentle squeeze, and then he was gone, the wrought iron gate closing with a soft clink behind him.

"*R*omeo and Juliet* isn't a *romance*, Miss Juliet. It's a *tragedy*."

"I beg your pardon, Lord Cross, but the entire play is about love and lovers, and the grief that befalls those who attempt to stand in the way of true love." Juliet Templeton grinned, enjoying every moment of Cross's irritation. "What could be more romantic than that?"

Johnathan cast a sidelong glance at Emmeline, as he now thought of her. She was seated on the carriage bench beside him, her bemused gaze focused on her sister's animated face as Juliet teased Cross.

She seemed hardly aware Johnathan was there, while he, meanwhile, was painfully aware of her. He was going mad, the warmth of her body so close beside his driving him to distraction.

It had been five days. Five days, a half-dozen calls, and two visits to private rose gardens near London, and neither of the Templeton sisters had given themselves away. He had no definitive proof that either Emmeline or Juliet was the Lady in Lavender.

But his heart, the same heart that had been

NOT JUST ANY EARL

turned inside out, told him the lady who'd walked with him in Lady Fosberry's garden yesterday, who'd spoken with such enthusiasm about her botanical work, who touched the roses with care and reverence *must* be the same lady who'd kissed him with such sweet passion.

He fingered the violet ribbon tucked into his waistcoat pocket. He'd carried it with him everywhere since that night in Lady Fosberry's library, but now with Emmeline here, tucked into the carriage beside him, he realized the ribbon didn't matter.

The ribbon, that bewitching perfume, the color of a ball gown—none of it mattered. They were distractions, meaningless in the face of what he felt merely by looking at her.

She was the lady he'd kissed that night. He'd never been more certain of anything in his life. Not because she'd confessed it, or because he'd learned anything new about the Lady in Lavender, but because his heart had only ever leapt from his chest for one lady; his knees had only ever weakened over one kiss.

He'd only ever felt the same desire and tenderness he did for Emmeline Templeton one time before: five nights ago, when he'd kissed a lady with a scent that belonged to her alone, the magical result of a subtle, elusive rose, mingled with the unique fragrance of her skin.

"*Hopeless* love, Miss Templeton." Cross rapped his walking stick on the floor of the carriage, recalling Johnathan's wandering attention. "A *star-crossed* love which leads to unspeakable tragedy. I'd as soon call *Othello* a romance as I would *Romeo and Juliet*."

"Don't be absurd, Lord Cross. *Othello* isn't about

love at all, but jealousy. Why, I can't think of anything less romantic than a jealous husband."

"My dear Juliet." Lady Fosberry looked up from settling her skirts. "A lady does not speak of jealous husbands to a gentleman."

"Next you'll try and persuade me *Macbeth* isn't a tragedy, despite the blood, murder, and death on every page." Cross's fingers twitched on the head of his walking stick as he gazed at Juliet Templeton in annoyance and grudging admiration.

"No, indeed." Juliet tossed her head. "It's certainly a tragedy, but not because of the blood or murders. It's a domestic tragedy, my lord, about man's impotence."

"*Juliet!*" Lady Fosberry gasped. "My dear, a lady *certainly* does not speak about anything having to do with a gentleman's potency—"

"*Impotency*, my lady—"

"Impotence!" Cross looked as if he were torn between horror and laughter, neither of which seemed as if it would do much to quell Juliet's high spirits. "Your contention, Miss Juliet, is that the tragedy arises not from Lady Macbeth's consuming ambition, but from Macbeth's impotence?"

"Oh, dear," Lady Fosberry muttered. "Perhaps I should have taken my own carriage."

"Of course, impotence." Juliet spoke as if she couldn't imagine what the fuss was about, given how perfectly obvious it was. "Well, that and the slow disintegration of a marriage as a metaphor for the disintegration of morality into lawlessness and evil."

Cross gaped at her as if she were some rare, exotic creature he'd never encountered before. "I fear Shakespeare would disagree with—"

"What can you tell us about Lady Hammond's roses, my lord?" Lady Fosberry turned to Johnathan with a bright smile. "Is her garden as impressive as it's said to be?"

"I believe so, yes, but I'm no judge of gardens. Her collection of damask roses is considered one of the finest in England, but I'll await Miss Templeton's opinion on that."

Johnathan glanced down at Emmeline. She'd been worrying her lower lip ever since Cross and Juliet began bickering, turning it a plump, distracting red.

He smothered a groan, and shifted slightly away from the slender curve of her thigh, which was pressed so snugly against his in the close confines of the carriage a shift in any direction on her part would make this drive a good deal more...potent.

"What a lovely day for a drive!" Juliet Templeton's lips curved in a winning smile. "Don't you agree, Lord Cross? Or are sunny days also a harbinger of tragedy?"

Cross merely grunted in reply, but he never took his eyes off Juliet for the remainder of the drive. When they arrived at Hammond Park and descended from the chaise, she took his arm with a playful smile. "Come, Lord Cross. Surely, you won't waste such a day as this? I've been longing to see Lady Hammond's climbing roses."

Cross's only reply was another grunt, but he allowed Juliet to lead him down one of the walkways. Lady Fosberry found a comfortable bench and focused her attention on keeping her skirts free of dust, while Johnathan drew Emmeline's hand through his arm and took her in the other direction, into a quiet corner of the grounds where the damask roses took pride of place.

They walked along in silence for a while, the only sound the birds and the crunch of their feet on the graveled pathway, until Emmeline paused to run her fingers over the ruffled edges of the petals of a bold, scarlet rose.

"Portland roses." She turned to him with a smile. "The Duchess of Portland brought this species back from the Continent. She was a botanist, and an avid collector. These are repeat-flowering roses, meaning they don't just bloom once, but multiple times before the frost."

"Does it have a scent?" Johnathan asked, drawing closer, hypnotized by the motion of her slender fingers caressing the delicate bloom.

"Oh, yes. Damask roses are wonderfully fragrant." Emmeline leaned down and brought her nose close to the tight cluster of roses.

Johnathan drew nearer still, until he was right beside her, his gaze on her bent head. "How would you describe this rose's scent?"

"Sweet, and feminine, and...flowery, though I suppose one could say the same of any flower." She let out a soft, self-deprecating laugh. "This one has a hint of lemon to it."

"Does it?" Johnathan leaned down, so their cheeks were mere inches apart, and inhaled. "Do you detect a touch of orange?"

Emmeline colored at his nearness, but she didn't shift away from him. Instead, she sampled the rose again, a faint crease appearing in her brow as she considered it. "It's subtle, but yes, I think so. You have a sensitive nose, my lord."

It was an odd compliment, but it gave him far more pleasure than being called the Nonesuch ever had. "No one's ever praised my nose before."

That coaxed a laugh from her, and she chattered about the diversity in scent among the various damask roses as they wandered through the garden. "Lady Hammond's rose gardens have been arranged with an eye to appearance, which is common among large, formal gardens, but if I had my own rose garden, I'd organize them by complimentary scent."

Johnathan smiled. "What, and allow a riot of competing colors? Pink roses next to red, and red next to orange? Shocking, Miss Templeton."

"I daresay it would be chaos, but beautiful still. Have you ever seen an ugly rose, my lord?" she asked, returning his easy grin.

"No, but have you ever smelled a rose that isn't sweet, Miss Templeton?"

"I have, in fact. Some roses have sharp, unpleasant fragrances, and others have an earthy, woody smell like moss, that many find offensive."

"But you don't?"

"I prefer some scents over others, but every rose has its place. Now, I don't say I wouldn't tuck the mossy roses into a more remote corner of my own garden."

Johnathan chuckled. "Some accommodation must be made for them, certainly, but surely you have no reason to wish for your own garden? When we visited Lady Finchley's roses, you mentioned a walled garden at your home in Buckinghamshire. Is it not yours to do with as you please?"

"It's...yes, I suppose it is mine now, as much as it is anyone's, but it was my father's garden, and a part of me will always regard it as his." She was quiet for some moments before murmuring, "It's greatly reduced from what it once was, I'm afraid."

"What happened to it?" He could guess, but he wanted to give her a chance to talk about it, if she chose.

"My father was ill for some time, after the—that is, before he died."

After...

Had she been about to say something about her mother's scandal? "Lady Christine, during her call yesterday...I never imagined she could be so cruel. I beg your pardon for her—"

"You have no need to beg my pardon for anything Lady Christine says, my lord. You were...what you said to her was...well, no one other than Lady Fosberry has ever spoken up on our behalf before." Emmeline cast him a look that made the breath catch in Johnathan's throat. "I never realized how much I'd always hoped someone would, until you did."

Johnathan tried to read her expression, but she'd turned her face up to the sky, and he could only gaze at her as patches of sunlight caressed her forehead and cheeks, her soft red lips, as lush and tempting as any rose.

"His garden was left untouched for nearly a year after he became ill. By the time I began tending it again, what hadn't withered from neglect was destroyed by pests and disease. It's gone, aside from a few of my father's hybrid roses, and I don't hold out much hope for them."

His throat tightened at the grief on her face, and he might have done something improper, like take her into his arms and press her sweet, lovely face to his chest, but then she added in a whisper, "The garden is only one of many ruins my mother left behind, Lord Melrose. A trail of wreckage followed in her wake."

Emmeline didn't seem to expect a reply, and indeed, there was little he could say, but he pressed her hand, desperate to reassure her somehow, to ease the sadness in her eyes.

She remained quiet as they wandered on, until they turned a corner and she came to a halt in the middle of the pathway with a gasp. "Oh, look, my lord! Aren't they lovely?"

Johnathan had been gazing down at the fingertips of her gloved hand resting on his sleeve and recalling the curl of slender fingers around the windowsill in Lady Fosberry's library, but when he glanced up his eyes widened. They'd somehow stumbled upon a private corner that surpassed every beauty that had come before, a tiny oasis tucked inside the sprawling garden.

A graceful, white stone temple stood at its center, and inside Johnathan glimpsed a sculpture of a lady in a flowing Grecian dress with a crown of white stone roses nestled on her head. A pair of benches flanked the temple, each carefully placed so the shadows cast by the columns protected them from the sun.

But the temple wasn't what had made Emmeline gasp.

It was the roses. Dozens upon dozens of them spilling from stone pots and trellises in a dazzling cascade of blooms. They were all of the same species, all of them such a faint, delicate pink the sunlight turned them translucent, as if the petals had been fashioned from the thinnest pearl white shells.

Emmeline seemed to be frozen in place, so Johnathan urged her forward until they were standing amidst the riotous tumble of roses. She turned in a circle, her smoky blue eyes wide, and for a moment he couldn't breathe, watching her.

The roses, the sunlight, the pure white stone—none of it could compare to her. She was the most beautiful thing in any garden, the most beautiful lady he'd ever seen.

"Do you..." Johnathan began, but he was obliged to clear the sudden hoarseness from his throat. "Do you know these roses?"

She turned to him, her lips curving in a smile of such pure delight he thought might fall to his knees for her.

Then, on the heels of that thought...

I already have.

"I've only seen them in a book, but I believe they're Baronet Hume's Blush Tea-Scented China roses. I've read about them, but they only bloomed in England for the first time about a decade ago, and I've never seen them growing in a garden before."

Her pleasure in the roses was contagious, and Johnathan found himself grinning like a fool. "And their scent? My guess is that it's reminiscent of tea."

"Yes, strongly of black tea. Come, shall we see for ourselves?" She grasped his hand, her long fingers tucked into his palm, and Johnathan followed after her, scolding his heart for beating with such wild hope at her touch when she didn't even seem aware she'd taken his hand.

She led him along behind her until they reached

the two benches, where a particularly lush spill of blooms nestled among a bed of bright green leaves. "Oh! They have a lovely scent, do they not?"

"A lovely scent, and wicked thorns." Johnathan cautiously fingered one of the stems. "Are the blooms very heavy? The head of the rose is bent, as if it's nodding off to sleep."

"Sleeping, or weeping, yes. See how thin the canes are? They're too weak to fully support the large, dense blooms, and so they weep."

Johnathan tipped up one of the nodding blooms, as if he were tipping up its chin, then let it nod again, a smile drifting across his lips. "Well, I can't say I approve of pouting, but they're charming this way, aren't they?"

"I can't imagine them any other way. What a joy, to have a chance to see them! The plates in my books don't do them justice." Emmeline traced a reverent finger around the edges of one of the blooms. "I'd love to have one to press. I don't imagine I'll get the chance to see one again."

"I'm certain Lady Hammond wouldn't mind sharing one of her roses with you." Johnathan waved a hand at the thick curtain of blossoms surrounding them. "She has plenty, as you can see."

"What, *steal* one of Lady Hammond's roses? I couldn't possibly do such a thing, and anyway, I couldn't bear to ruin one by cutting it."

"We don't need to cut one. There must be a few that have fallen...ah, yes." Johnathan bent and retrieved several blooms that had dropped from the trellis to the ground. "Here, you may have your choice."

ANNA BRADLEY

Emmeline bit her lip. "Is it truly all right, do you suppose?"

"Yes, I do." Johnathan held out the roses, and after a little hesitation, she plucked one from his palm.

He raised the other to his nose, inhaling deeply, and the spicy scent of black tea filled his head. "There's another scent there, but I can't identify it. Is it some sort of fruit?"

He brought the rose close to her face, holding it steady while her pert little nose—which was quite the most adorable nose he'd ever seen—twitched delicately. Her cheeks were flushed with sunshine and pleasure, and her lips parted as the scent of black tea filled the air between them, as if she were tasting the scent on her tongue.

Desire pooled in his belly, his stomach muscles tightening at the warm pulse of it, his limbs going heavy and lazy as he watched her from under half-lowered lids.

"Citrus, I think, or perhaps..." She trailed off as her eyes met his. A blush colored her cheeks and rushed down the long line of her neck.

"Perhaps?" Johnathan's gaze followed that bewitching blush, and settled on the pulse fluttering in the soft, tempting hollow of her throat.

Dear God, he could become obsessed with her neck, her throat—

"Perhaps...raspberry?" she whispered, swiping her tongue across her bottom lip.

Gently, he brushed the delicate petals of the rose in his hand across her lips, and stifled a groan as they parted further.

"Raspberry?" *Yes.* Plump, sweet red raspberries.

Was it the hint of raspberries that stole his reason, or the dainty pucker of her lips as they formed the word, or the scent of the roses, black tea and raspberry and some exotic spice he couldn't name spiraling through his veins? Or was it simply *her*, her blue eyes touched with silvery gray like a winter sea, widening as he drew closer, the uncertain flutter of her dark lashes as they lowered, then lifted again, holding his gaze as he cradled her cheeks in his palms.

My hands are shaking...

It was all of these things, or perhaps none of them, but in the next breath it no longer mattered, because he was kissing her, and she was opening for him, her mouth soft and giving, one small, gloved hand reaching for him, her fingers warm through the thin cotton as they rested against his neck.

The innocent touch nearly undid him. *"Emmeline."*

Her only reply was a soft sigh, the warm drift of her breath teasing his senses and stealing his own breath, and he knew—in an instant, he knew it was *her* kiss that had been haunting him since that night in Lady Fosberry's library. *Her* kiss that had transformed him, because he was no longer the same man he'd been before he found her.

He would never be that man again—never *wanted* to be that man who'd believed he could live a lifetime without knowing what it felt like to kiss Emmeline Templeton.

She shifted closer, turning toward him, her skirts brushing his legs, and he slid his palm down her shoulder, his thumb dragging over her collarbones, until he settled it at her waist, so he might keep her close.

~

ALL EMMELINE COULD SEE WAS Johnathan—because yes, he was *Johnathan* to her now, had ceased to be Lord Melrose days ago—and all she could feel was the tickle of rose petals against her lips, his mouth hovering over hers before he took it a kiss that flooded her with warmth, from her spinning head to her curling toes.

Every thought in her brain fled, but for one.

I want to dive into that warmth, press my face into his chest, and remain there forever.

He kissed her tenderly, but with an insistence that hinted at restrained passion, his tongue teasing at the seam of her lips until she opened for him with a soft moan. A low, fierce growl rumbled in his chest as he plunged inside, his tongue stroking hers until the garden spun around Emmeline in a whirl of dizzying desire.

When he drew away, they were both breathless. "Look at me, Emmeline."

Emmeline shook her head, her eyes squeezed tightly closed, like a child trying to escape a scolding, because if she looked at him, if she looked into those devastating blue eyes and found that same tenderness with which he'd gazed at her in the garden yesterday, she'd be lost to him forever.

"Yes." He touched a gentle finger to her chin, raising her face to his so he could look into her eyes. "Look at me."

Oh, she didn't want to! She was afraid of him, and of herself and everything she felt when she was with him, but his voice was so soft and coaxing, his fingers stroking her skin so gently, she could refuse him nothing.

"Your eyes were the first thing I noticed about you. Beautiful. I should have known it at once, as soon as I saw your eyes."

A trembling began deep in Emmeline's belly. "Known, my lord?"

Johnathan's eyes darkened. "Are you cold, sweetheart?"

Sweetheart. Dear God. Words felt too difficult just then, so she shook her head.

He rested his hand on her waist, the warmth seeping through his glove and leaving an imprint of his palm against her ribs. "I can feel you shivering."

"I...not from the cold." It wasn't what she meant to say—it was much too honest, much more than she'd intended to reveal, but he'd disarmed her some-how, her natural wariness no match for him.

Perhaps it was his eyes, the kindness in them.

"Do I make you shiver, Emmeline?" he whispered, resting his forehead against hers.

Emmeline's lips parted, but all that emerged was a soft sigh.

His gaze darted to her lips, "Have you ever kissed a gentleman before?"

"No. I—I don't know any gentlemen."

But she *had* kissed a gentleman—*this* gentleman, and everything inside her urged her to tell him, to confess she was the lady he'd kissed in the library, that she was the Lady in Lavender.

He knows. He already knows...

"Ah. You may not realize, then, how much a kiss can reveal. Secrets, truths one might wish to keep hidden all disintegrate in the wake of a truly breathtaking kiss." He dragged his thumb gently over her bottom lip, a flush rising in his cheeks when she parted for him. "Do you know what I learned from your kiss, Emmeline?"

"No," she whispered.

"That I've kissed you once before." He urged her closer, so close he was cradling her against the firm, muscular wall of his chest. "This isn't our first kiss, is it, sweetheart?"

Emmeline tried to look away, ashamed of the secrets she'd kept, the lies she'd told.

Ashamed of her cowardice.

But Johnathan wouldn't allow it. He kept her face tipped up to his with a nudge of his fingertips as he reached into his coat pocket and pulled out a bit of violet silk. "This belongs to you, doesn't it?"

"My ribbon." Emmeline cast him a shy look from under her lashes. "I thought it was lost forever."

"I've kept this ribbon in my pocket since that night in Lady Fosberry's library. When I saw you at Floris with that bit of linen with the same lingering scent, I thought the Lady in Lavender must be either you or your sister. I, ah...haven't conducted myself as a gentleman ought to, but you must believe me, Emmeline, when I say I not only believed you were the lady I'd kissed, but *wished* it with all my heart."

Emmeline gazed down at the ribbon between his fingers for a long time before raising her eyes once again to his face, losing herself in blue eyes the color of cornflowers.

His dear, handsome face.

Weeks ago, Lady Fosberry had told her he was just the gentleman to surprise them all, and he *had* surprised her. He hadn't behaved in a way she could possibly have predicted, but that wasn't what truly stunned Emmeline.

It was that *she* hadn't.

Her last fleeting thought before his lips took hers again was how strange it was that *she*—shy, dull Emmeline, a spinster in the making in her dusty pinafores, the bluestocking with her nose forever pressed between the pages of a book...

That *she*, of all people, would prove to be the most unpredictable of them all.

CHAPTER
ELEVEN

"Will this do for the theater?" Juliet turned away from the looking glass to face Emmeline, the skirts of her opera gown drifting around her ankles.

Emmeline looked up, and a smile of pure pleasure curved her lips. Not one lady in a dozen could do justice to evening primrose, but the rich yellow hue brought out Juliet's dark, dramatic beauty. "You look lovely. That color is perfect for you."

"I suppose it will do." Juliet straightened the neckline of her gown, a smile lighting up her own face as she caught Emmeline's reflection in the glass. "My, how pretty you look tonight, Emmeline!"

"Do I?" Emmeline glanced down at herself, surprised, and smoothed her damp palms down her rose-colored silk skirt.

"Of course. You always do. The lace on that gown is exquisite, and you've such a tiny waist." Juliet tugged on her gloves, her gaze meeting Emmeline's in the glass. "I daresay Lord Melrose won't be able to take his eyes off you."

Emmeline had been fussing with her skirts, but at this her eyes flew to Juliet's. She opened her mouth to insist Lord Melrose had never spared her a glance, but this and a dozen other denials didn't make it past her lips.

Because they were lies, and Emmeline was, at last, finished with lies.

Particularly the lies she'd told herself.

She'd been wrong about love from the start. How she'd ever imagined she could be *right* about it was a mystery, given she'd never experienced it, but while inexperience was forgivable, it wasn't as easy to excuse her arrogance in thinking it was *her* place to orchestrate matches as if she were arranging roses in tidy, predictable rows.

Lady Fosberry had warned Phee that people were nothing like numbers, and as it happened, they were nothing like roses, either.

The truth was, things had been careening wildly out of control since that night in Lady Fosberry's library, like a runaway horse that flew in whatever direction it liked, without any regard for the people in its path, or the rider on its back.

For all Emmeline's knowledge of botany, all her scientific theories and her plans and machinations, the only thing she'd ever been able to do was hold on and hope for the best. It was all any of them could do.

"I am fond of this color," Juliet was saying as she inspected her reflection.

Emmeline cocked her head as she studied Juliet in the glass, recalling the expression on her sister's face when she'd been arguing with Lord Cross about Shakespeare's tragedies.

There'd been something there, something Emmeline had never seen before, but her vivacious, spirited sister with the somber, unsmiling Lord Cross? In a thousand years she never would have put the two of them together, but then she'd proven herself to be hopelessly inept when it came to matters of the heart. "I think...I think Lord Cross admires you, Juliet."

Juliet let out a tinkling laugh. "Lord Cross is far too irascible to admire anyone."

Emmeline blinked. Well, that didn't *sound* much like love, but...

"Do you admire *him*?"

"Yes, but only because it amuses me to foil his efforts to offend everyone. I've never seen a man more determined to thwart admiration than Lord Cross."

Juliet shrugged, but it didn't escape Emmeline's notice that she hadn't answered the question, and her cheeks had gone a deep pink. Emmeline said nothing, but a cautious smile rose to her lips as they made their way down the stairs to the waiting carriage.

Perhaps, just perhaps, the Templeton's fortunes were finally changing.

～

"MY GOODNESS, Emmeline, do stop flailing about, won't you, dear? That's the third time you've trod on me since we left for the theater." Lady Fosberry tugged on the hem of her gown to coax it out from under Emmeline's foot.

"I beg your pardon." Emmeline hastily tucked her feet under her chair, her cheeks heating. Since they'd arrived at Covent Garden Theater, she'd been so preoccupied with searching for a golden head atop a pair of broad shoulders it was a wonder she hadn't tumbled from their box.

"What is everyone gossiping about?" Juliet whispered, glancing at the surrounding boxes. "The *ton*'s got some delicious tidbit between their teeth, and they've been gnawing on it since we arrived. Has something happened? If it has, please tell me at once. I can't bear any more surprises."

"Nothing's happened, dearest. I'd know if it had." Lady Fosberry gave Juliet's hand a reassuring pat.

"You may be sure something's happened. The muttering is positively deafening. We seem to be the only ones who don't know what it is. Oh, I don't like this at all."

Emmeline shivered in her rose silk gown, rubbing her bare arms to chase away a sudden chill. They'd arrived early, and a great many of the boxes were still empty, but in the box beside theirs sat a gray-haired lady she didn't recognize, her head bent toward a younger companion who was seated beside her. The first lady's lips were moving rapidly as she whispered something into her friend's ear, and both of their faces were alight with ill-concealed delight.

She recognized that expression, that look of vicious glee.

Juliet was right. The *ton* was aflutter over some rumor, and if she could judge by the rising whispers, it was spreading like a contagion.

Dear God, what now?

She stilled, straining to catch a word here or there, praying with everything inside her she wouldn't hear anything about Lord Melrose or the Lady in Lavender, and paralyzed with dread that she would.

Juliet snapped open her fan, and ducked behind

it. "There's another scandal afoot, you may be certain of it."

"I do believe you're right, Juliet. Stay here, girls, while I go and find out what it is." Lady Fosberry nodded toward the gray-haired lady in the neighboring box. "Lady Browning and her daughter are just there, and they're both dreadful gossips. I'll have the whole of it soon enough, I promise you."

Emmeline's heart rushed into her throat, and before she knew what she was doing, her hand snaked out to stop Lady Fosberry. "Please don't, my lady! Perhaps it's best if we stay out of it this time."

"It's much too late for that, I'm afraid. It's best if we know what it is at once." Lady Fosberry gently pried the folds of her skirt from Emmeline's fingers. "My dear, why do you suppose we came tonight? Not to hear Juliet Capulet chatter about love from her bedchamber balcony, I assure you."

"But—"

"At worst, it's something regarding poor Lord Melrose's predicament. At best, a new scandal's afoot, and the *ton* has moved on from the Lady in Lavender. We can only hope it's the latter." Lady Fosberry rose from her seat with a sigh. "Dear me, this season has quite soured me on gossip."

"But I don't think—"

It was too late, however. Lady Fosberry was already gone. She appeared in the neighboring box, and Lady Browning tugged her down into an empty seat and began a furious whispering.

"For pity's sake," Juliet hissed. "Does Lady Browning imagine she's being quiet, with that flapping tongue? They can likely hear her down in the pit!"

"Hush! I'm trying to listen." Emmeline laid a hand on Juliet's arm to quiet her. "I can't quite tell what all the fuss is, but Lady Browning said something about...Lord Cudworth. Yes, I'm certain she said something about Lord Cudworth."

Dear God, what awful lies had spewed from his lips *this* time?

"She just said something about Lady Christine Dingley. Goodness, Lady Browning can go on, and none of it to the purpose," Juliet muttered from behind her fan. "I wonder how Lady Fosberry hasn't choked it out of her by now."

Lord Cudworth, and Lady Christine? A shudder tripped down Emmeline's spine. No good ever came from those two.

"Wait! Lady Browning just mentioned Lord Melrose." Juliet gripped Emmeline's arm. "Of course, she's chosen *now* to lower her voice, the maddening thing, but it's something to do with Lord Melrose, Lord Cudworth, and Lady Christine Dingley. Oh, dear, that doesn't sound promising, does it?"

Lady Fosberry came rushing back into their box then, looking pale and grim. "Well, my dears, it isn't good news. The *ton* hasn't moved onto another scandal."

Emmeline clutched at the arms of her chair with numb fingers. "What do you mean, my lady?"

"Lady Christine Dingley and Lord Cudworth are betrothed." Lady Fosberry nodded toward a box one level above theirs, and to their right. Lady Christine was seated in the first row, wearing an ice blue gown, sapphires flashing at her ears and throat, and beside her sat Lord Cudworth, elegant in his black evening dress, a proprietary hand on Lady Christine's arm.

"That's not all. It's, ah...well, it's very bad, dearests." Lady Fosberry's voice was faint. "It seems Lord Cudworth has once again changed his mind about the Lady in Lavender."

"What *now*?" Juliet threw up her hands. "Was she wearing indigo this time? Or lilac, perhaps?"

"Violet." Lady Fosberry's voice shook. "Violet silk, and he claims she has chestnut-colored hair."

Emmeline stared at her, her stomach clenching with dread.

But no, it couldn't be. Even Lady Christine couldn't be so cruel as to—

"Chestnut hair? But he said before it was too dark to see the lady! How can he know what color her hair —" Juliet broke off as she glanced up at the Dingley's box and saw Lady Dingley, Lady Christine, and Lord Cudworth all smirking down at them with spiteful triumph.

The becoming pink color drained from Juliet's cheeks. "Why, that wicked, devious, sneaking thing! I suppose they've run to every drawing room in London with my name on their lips, haven't they?"

Lady Fosberry opened her mouth, then closed it again, but her despairing expression told them everything, without her having to say a word.

"But how can anyone take anything Lord Cudworth says as the truth? He's told a half-dozen different stories already. Now he's decided Juliet is the Lady in Lavender? Why, anyone can see the Dingley's have put him up to this!"

But even as the words left her lips, Emmeline knew it was hopeless. The *ton* didn't care for the truth, only for scandal. Surely, she should have learned that lesson by now?

She followed Juliet's stricken gaze as it moved over the rows of boxes flanking either side of the stage, the bright lights in each illuminating the company seated inside. More people had streamed in and taken their places in their boxes, and every one of them seemed to be staring at them, some craning their necks to get a better look, all of them whispering and snickering.

Emmeline raised a shaking hand to her mouth. This was her worst nightmare come to life, and it was unfolding right here in Lady Fosberry's box, with the entire *ton* looking on.

Only this time, it was worse. This time, they'd caught Juliet in their sights.

What have I done?

"Quickly, girls." Lady Fosberry snatched up her wrap, her voice barely above a whisper. "Gather your things. We'll return home at once, and await Lord Melrose."

Johnathan. Dear God, what must he be thinking?

Covent Garden Theatre was filled to the rafters by now, each of the boxes bursting at its seams with grinning *ton*, and their breathless attention seemed to be fixed, almost to a one, on Juliet.

Walking out of that theater with every eye upon them was one of the most difficult things Emmeline had ever done, but Juliet held her head high, defiance flashing in her blue eyes, and a pride so fierce surged through Emmeline she was able to keep her own chin up, and her eyes clear.

∼

"Lady Quigley is gawking at you through her quizzing glass." Cross nodded at a box several rows away. "Look at her. She's nearly falling off her chair, trying to get a better look. It would serve her right if she toppled over the edge."

"If she did, at least it would give the *ton* something else to talk about." The gossips hadn't yet wearied of Johnathan and the Lady in Lavender. If anything, they were more frenzied than ever, their gazes picking over him, buzzards searching for a bit of raw flesh.

He turned and glanced toward Lady Fosberry's box, a frown rising to his lips when he saw it was empty. He'd seen her ladyship there just moments before, with Emmeline and Juliet beside her, Emmeline more lovely than he'd ever seen her in a rose-colored gown that flattered her delicate complexion.

There was no time to dwell on it, however, because a few moments later, the curtain rose, and the performance began. Cross turned his attention to the stage, and Johnathan, determined not to give the *ton* anything more to gossip about, did his best to focus on the quarrel between the Montagues and Capulets.

Romeo and Juliet, of all morbid things. Ill-fated lovers, poison, and death. He didn't believe in such things as ill omens, or he might have imagined his own love affair was doomed.

As it was, he had more pleasant things to think about, and he fell into a vivid reverie of a petite lady with chestnut hair, her skin scented with roses, wrapped in delicate layers of lavender silk like a gift created for him alone.

If he'd been less preoccupied with waking dreams

of Emmeline's soft lips and silky skin, or if Cross had been the sort of gentleman to notice anything at all, they might have realized the chatter in the theater was growing louder with every passing moment, but finally, it reached such a fever pitch at the end of the first act even Cross couldn't fail to notice it. "For God's sake, what the devil is everyone nattering on about this time? I can't hear a bloody word Mercutio is say—"

By this point, the gossip had spread like wildfire, and Cross broke off, mouth agape. "Hell, and damnation. Something's amiss, Melrose."

Given his delicious musings, Johnathan might not have troubled himself much with Cross's grumbling. But there was an odd, choked note in his friend's voice that forced his eyes open, and he found the entire theater, from the deepest depths of the pit to the loftiest aristocrats in their private boxes, were buzzing about the Lady in Lavender.

Except this time, the lady had a name.

Juliet Templeton.

Not *Emmeline* Templeton, the lady he'd kissed with such passion among the blush pink roses yesterday. Not *Emmeline* Templeton, who'd admitted at last that *she* was the Lady in Lavender, *she* the lady he'd kissed and caressed so intimately in Lady Fosberry's library.

Not *Emmeline* Templeton, the lady he'd fallen madly in love with.

"It seems the *ton* has discovered the identity of the Lady in Lavender," Cross said slowly, his tone hollow.

Johnathan's hands curled into fists as his shock gave way to fury. "They haven't discovered a bloody thing. As usual, they've got it all wrong. I've never kissed Juliet Templeton in my life."

"Are you certain, Melrose? Are you absolutely *certain* Juliet Templeton isn't the Lady in Lavender?"

Johnathan opened his mouth to say yes, that he knew it without a shadow of doubt because Emmeline had told him that *she* was the Lady in Lavender, *she* was the lady who'd stolen his heart with one secret kiss, when all at once it occurred to him that she...

Hadn't.

He went back over their conversation yesterday, frantically searching for a single moment when a word of confession had fallen from her lips. He'd asked if he'd kissed her before, he'd asked if the violet ribbon belonged to her, and she'd said...

I thought it was lost forever.

That was all. She'd kissed him with an aching, familiar sweetness, but she'd never answered the question, never confessed in so many words that she was the Lady in Lavender.

Johnathan turned to Cross, sudden doubt gnawing at him. "I...no. No, I can't be absolutely certain."

At any other time, at any other moment Johnathan would have noticed at once that Cross's characteristically bland expression had vanished, but it was all happening too quickly now for him to make any sense of anything. He knew only the whispers were growing louder, and that his and Juliet Templeton's names were on every pair of lips.

At that moment, he would gladly have traded places with Romeo.

After he swallows the poison.

Instinctively he turned his livid gaze toward the Dingley's box, only to find Lady Christine watching him, a cold, venomous smile curling her lips.

She'd promised revenge, and she'd gotten it.

He and Cross left the theater before the start of the second act, the *ton*'s stares following them out, their whispers ringing in Johnathan's ears.

CHAPTER
TWELVE

An oppressive silence followed Emmeline, Lady Fosberry, and Juliet from Covent Garden Theater to her ladyship's carriage, and from the carriage through the entryway and into the drawing room beyond.

It wasn't until they were seated in front of the fire that Lady Fosberry ventured to speak, her expression dazed as it moved between Juliet and Emmeline. "Well, my dears. I never imagined when we left for the theater this evening that *we'd* become the performance."

Emmeline dropped onto a settee, her ears still burning. They'd left before the end of the first act, scurrying away like thieves in the night, but their departure hadn't quieted the wagging tongues. By then, the damage was already done.

Dear God, Juliet's expression when she'd seen Lady Christine's smug face...

"Juliet, dearest?" Lady Fosberry paused in front of the settee where Juliet sat, her back straight, her gaze on her lap. "If you've been keeping any secrets from

NOT JUST ANY EARL

me, now is the time for you to confess them. What do you have to say for yourself?"

Juliet startled when Lady Fosberry spoke, as if she'd forgotten anyone else was in the room. "I, ah...I hardly know what to say, my lady."

"It's all Lady Christine's doing, of course." Lady Fosberry began to pace from one end of the drawing room to the other, wringing her hands. "Lady Christine and her spiteful mother, and that ridiculous Lord Cudworth. Chestnut hair, indeed! If he can't distinguish lavender from periwinkle, or periwinkle from violet, why should anyone think he knows chestnut from sable, or sable from mahogany?"

"I don't understand it, my lady." Emmeline gave a helpless shake of her head. "He's changed his mind a dozen times. Why does anyone listen to him?" For all his smirking tonight, Lord Cudworth had failed to properly identify the color or purpose of the gown, as well as the lady wearing it, yet the *ton* had seized on Juliet's name as if every word out of his mouth was sacred truth.

"Why believe the truth when a lie is so much more entertaining?" Juliet was frozen in place, all but her hands, which she was clenching into fists until her knuckles whitened. "The *ton* must have their amusement, mustn't they, my lady?"

"Juliet, my dear, I must hear that it *is* a lie from your own lips." Lady Fosberry struggled for a moment, as if she'd rather choke on her next words than say them aloud. "Did you...you, and Lord Melrose... are you indeed the Lady in Lavender?"

Juliet let out a laugh, but there was a sharp, ugly edge to it. "You heard Lord Cudworth, my lady. It's the Lady in Violet now."

The bitterness in that laugh, the anger and hurt Juliet was trying so valiantly to hide cut Emmeline to the heart. What an utter fool she'd been, to believe the Templetons couldn't be ruined a second time. How laughable it was, to think the *ton* ever forgot or forgave anything.

Lady Fosberry pressed a weary hand to her brow. "We need to think what's best to do, girls. It's only a matter of time before your name will be on the lips of every gossip in London, Juliet."

"Oh, I daresay it already is." Juliet, who'd stuffed herself into the furthest corner of the settee, didn't meet either Emmeline's or Lady Fosberry's eyes. "Or it will be, before the end of the second act."

Lady Fosberry joined Juliet on the settee, taking her hand. "Juliet, dearest, I won't be angry with you, but I must know if you—"

"Lord Cudworth is mistaken, my lady." Juliet raised her chin, but she couldn't hide the trembling of her lips, the defeat written into every line of her face. "I'm not the Lady in Lavender."

Lady Fosberry's eyes slid closed as she let out a long breath. "No, I thought you couldn't be. You must forgive me for asking, dearest, but—"

"It doesn't matter now." Emmeline's voice was dull. "It doesn't matter if she's the Lady in Lavender or not. The truth doesn't matter."

Lady Fosberry blanched at the expression on Emmeline's face. "Emmeline, my dear girl, it's—"

"Juliet's done nothing wrong, but her innocence won't make a bit of difference to the *ton*. Soon enough they'll all be saying she intentionally lured Lord Melrose into an indiscretion so he'd be forced to marry her."

They'd say that, and worse. They'd claim Juliet was just like their mother had been, every inch a devious Templeton, and from there it would go on and on, the lies and innuendos piling up until the truth was crushed under their weight.

"I grant you the situation is dire, Emmeline," Lady Fosberry said with a quiet sigh. "But I can assure you I have no intention of allowing Lady Christine and Lord Cudworth to get away with such a horrendous lie."

"They've already gotten away with it. As Juliet said, it's such an amusing lie! Isn't that all that matters? Everyone in that theater tonight knows Lord Cudworth is lying about Juliet, just as they know Lady Christine put him up to it, but that won't keep them from repeating it all over London." She was rambling, but she couldn't seem to stop herself. "The truth is a dull, tedious thing, though in this case it might be shocking enough to satisfy even the *ton*."

"The truth?" Lady Fosberry paled at Emmeline's words. "God in heaven, what now? What do you mean, Emmeline? What *is* the truth? I must insist on knowing the whole of this business this instant."

"I should have told you at once. I beg your pardon, my lady, for lying to you." Emmeline rose slowly to her feet, her knees trembling. "I was the lady in the library with Lord Melrose the night of your ball. I'm the Lady in Lavender, Lady Fosberry. Not Juliet, but me."

Whatever Lady Fosberry had expected to hear, it wasn't *that*, and her jaw dropped right into her decolletage. "*You?* But...I don't understand. You weren't even at the ball! How could you and Lord Melrose have—"

Emmeline's face felt stiff, her lips numb. "I wasn't at the ball, no, but I *did* venture into the library in search of a book that night. Lord Melrose happened to come in when I was there, and...I didn't intend to... my encounter with his lordship was a mistake, my lady."

If she'd been any less devastated, Emmeline might have laughed that the odd chain of circumstances that had led to that kiss could be called a mistake. It felt far more like fate, a sequence of unlikely occurrences that would nevertheless change the entire course of her life.

Indeed, it already had.

She was in love with Johnathan. Perhaps she had been from that first moment he'd touched her in the library, and now...that would never *not* be true. How could anything ever be the same as it had been before that kiss, when *she* would never again be the same person she was before she fell in love with him?

"Of course it was, dearest. I could never think otherwise." Thankfully, Lady Fosberry didn't demand to know how Emmeline could have kissed Lord Melrose by *mistake*, but only gave her hand a gentle pat. "There's only one thing for it, then, and that's to tell Lord Melrose the truth at once."

"He already knows." He'd known almost from the start. All that time she'd been telling herself he didn't recognize her as the lady he'd kissed, he'd been quietly watching her, and drawing his own conclusions.

All the correct conclusions, as it happened.

But that only made it more painful. If she could have made herself believe Johnathan felt only a responsibility to the Lady in Lavender rather than a particular regard for *her*, she might someday have recovered from the loss of him.

But he'd *seen* her in a way no one ever had before, and now her heart was wholly, irretrievably his.

Lady Fosberry saw her distress, and an anxious frown creased her brow. "I don't understand why you didn't tell me at once. Would it really be so terrible, Emmeline, to be the Countess of Melrose?"

"I'm not destined to become a countess." Wasn't that what she'd told herself? That she was the flaw, the mistake that should have been corrected before the experiment even began?

How absurd, to think it could be done as easily as that.

"Nonsense, Emmeline. You'd make a splendid countess, and then there's the small matter of your being the lady Lord Melrose is searching for."

"But—"

"Give me a moment, please, girls." Lady Fosberry held up a hand to silence Emmeline, who'd opened her mouth to speak. "Just a moment to think, and I'm sure I'll come up with some way to—"

The drawing room door opened then, startling all three of them. "I beg your pardon, my lady," Watkins said with a bow. "Lord Melrose has just arrived."

Lady Fosberry blew out a breath. "Yes, we've been expecting him. Show him in, Watkins."

Juliet remained as she was, only the quick dart of her gaze toward the door betraying her nerves, but Emmeline dropped back down onto the settee, her heart crawling into her throat at the mention of Johnathan's name.

A moment later he stormed into the drawing room, his hair disheveled and his eyes wild, looking as if he'd run straight from Covent Garden to Hampstead Heath.

"My dear Lord Melrose, I think we—" Lady Fosberry began.

But Johnathan didn't seem aware Lady Fosberry or Juliet were even in the room. He strode over to the settee where Emmeline sat, and gathered her hands in his. "Emmeline."

Her treacherous heart melted at the sound of her name on his lips, and dear God, she didn't know what to say, or where to look, nor could she bring herself to withdraw her hands from his.

Lady Fosberry didn't share Emmeline's hesitation. "It seems we've discovered the identity of the Lady in Lavender at last, my lord. Unfortunately, this situation has become a good deal more complicated than either of us could have anticipated."

"On the contrary, my lady. The truth is simple." Johnathan's fingers tightened around Emmeline's, squeezing gently. "After our conversation among Lady Hammond's roses yesterday, I was left with the impression *you* are the Lady in Lavender, but you never actually said so."

It occurred to Emmeline then that she could lie, and claim she hadn't said so because she *wasn't* the Lady in Lavender, but even if she'd wanted to, she could never look into Johnathan's eyes and lie to him.

"I came to beg for the truth from your lips." Johnathan gazed at her with hope burning in his cornflower-blue eyes. "But I already know the truth, Emmeline."

If she looked into his eyes again, she'd burst into tears, so Emmeline looked away, gazing blindly at a point over his shoulder. "The truth no longer matters, my lord. Half the *ton* witnessed the spectacle at the theater tonight, and the other half will know every detail of it by breakfast tomorrow morning."

"It hardly matters? How can it not matter? Look at me, Emmeline." Johnathan turned her face toward his, so she had no choice but to meet his eyes. "*You* are the lady I kissed that night in the library, and *you* are the lady I've fallen in love with. That is the *only* thing that matters."

Oh, how Emmeline wished that were true!

"Emmeline Templeton." Johnathan raised her hand to his lips. "I humbly beg..."

Lady Fosberry gasped, her hand flying to her heart, but Emmeline could only stare at Johnathan, speechless.

Surely, he didn't mean to—

"For the honor of your hand..."

He *did* mean to do it, *was* doing it, even now. She remained silent, her mind racing.

"...proper courtship, and the wedding as soon as possible, before the end of the season."

Courtship, he'd said. He was talking about a betrothal, a wedding, a marriage...

Emmeline smothered the sob on her lips at the earnestness with which he declared himself, the warmth in his eyes. He was so handsome, but even his beauty paled in comparison to his goodness. There wasn't one man in a hundred with the honor to offer for her under the circumstances, but he was offering her his hand and his heart without reservation.

And she had no choice but to break his heart, and her own, with a refusal. "I—forgive me, my lord, but a marriage between us is out of the question now.

Surely you see that Juliet must become the Countess of Melrose?"

"*Me?*" Juliet repeated in astonishment.

"Juliet?" Lady Fosberry echoed, as if she'd misheard. "But *you're* the Lady in Lavender, Emmeline. What has Juliet got to do with it?"

"Juliet is the lady all of London *believes* to be the Lady in Lavender." Emmeline's heart gave a despairing wrench in her chest. "The only way to put this right again is for Johnathan and Juliet to marry. Otherwise, Juliet's reputation will be forever ruined."

"Emmeline!" Lady Fosberry exclaimed. "I beg you to consider—"

"There's nothing to consider." Emmeline resisted the urge to drop her head into her hands and instead forged ahead, desperate to have this done. "I'm responsible for this mess, and I won't leave Juliet to suffer for my mistakes in my place."

Juliet was staring at her, her eyes enormous in her pale face. "You'd toss away your chance at happiness to...what, Emmeline? Appease the *ton*? Satisfy Lord Cudworth, a man willing to destroy another lady's reputation so he can have Lady Christine Dingley's fortune?"

"No. Not for any of those reasons, but for *you*, Juliet. Do you suppose I'll pursue my own happiness at your expense?" Emmeline gripped Juliet's hand, desperate to make her understand how terrible it was to be caught in the *ton*'s web without any hope of escape, how like being a helpless fly at the mercy of a spider it was.

How *lonely* it was.

The thought of her lovely, bright sister humiliated by the *ton* and sent back to Hambleden Manor with a devastating scandal attached to her name made bile rise in Emmeline's throat.

Not this time. Not Juliet.

"*No*, Emmeline." Tears stood in Juliet's eyes even as they blazed with defiance. "This is nonsense. I won't allow you to sacrifice your happiness for me."

"What happens to you, Juliet, once I seize my happiness? You won't be able to set foot in London without fearing the *ton*'s scorn! Every time you walk down a street, you'll hear them whispering about you behind your back! No. I won't have it. A marriage between you and Lord Melrose will silence the wagging tongues, and it's the only thing that will."

"Am I to have any say in which lady I marry, Emmeline?" Johnathan demanded, his calmness deserting him. "Or have you made the decision for all of us?"

"I can only make the decision for myself, my lord, and so I have. I—I must refuse you, my lord. I can't become your countess."

Johnathan was staring at her like a man who was struggling to keep his head above water, only to realize the undertow was going to take him, regardless. "This is madness, Emmeline. You must see that!"

Emmeline tried to smile as she reached out to press her palm to Johnathan's cheek. "It's for the best. I'd make a dreadful countess, whereas Juliet was born to—"

Without warning, Johnathan's hand snaked out, grabbing her wrist. "Do you truly think it's that simple, Emmeline? That I can exchange one sister for the other, and go on as if I haven't lost the lady I love?"

"Johnathan—" Emmeline whispered, stricken.

"No." Johnathan's eyes were a dark, stormy blue,

glittering with anger and despair. "What happens when the *ton* realizes Lady Christine and Lord Cudworth are lying, that you're the Lady in Lavender, and not Juliet? Because they will, Emmeline. The truth always finds a way to make itself known."

Emmeline had no answer for that. She knew only that with every word from his mouth her resistance was crumbling. If she remained in this room, soon enough she'd give him everything he asked for, everything she had.

Gently, she withdrew her wrist from his grasp. "I beg I may be excused, my lady."

Lady Fosberry hesitated, but then gave a weary nod. "We've all had a bit of a shock. I think it's best if we resume this discussion tomorrow, when cooler heads prevail. Go up to your bedchamber, Emmeline. Lord Melrose, I invite you to call on us tomorrow morning. Perhaps we can persuade Emmeline to see reason then."

Emmeline said nothing, but by the time Johnathan arrived tomorrow, she'd be gone. As long as she remained here, he'd never reconcile himself to a marriage with Juliet.

Johnathan exhaled in a quick, sharp breath, but after a long look at Emmeline, he took up his hat, and offered them all a stiff bow. "Until tomorrow, then."

There wouldn't be a tomorrow. She'd return to Buckinghamshire as soon as the sun rose, and she'd go alone. Lady Fosberry wouldn't like it—she'd attempt to talk Emmeline out of it—but when she realized it was useless, she'd let her go.

Emmeline waited until she heard the sound of Johnathan's carriage in the drive, then she dragged herself upstairs, more exhausted than she could ever remember being in her life before.

The Hambleden Glory hadn't yet bloomed, and she'd never found the damask rose she needed to complete her father's perfume. Hadn't that been all that mattered to her, once? Now she was leaving London as empty-handed as she'd arrived.

No, more so, because she was leaving her heart behind.

THIRTEEN

Johnathan had slept very ill last night. Each time he closed his eyes he imagined the *ton* as they'd been last night at the theater, the avid, greedy expressions on their faces, their mouths spewing one lie after the next.

The first lie had come straight from the lips of Lady Christine and Lord Cudworth—that it had been Juliet Templeton fleeing the library the night of Lady Fosberry's ball, her violet silk gown askew—but the *ton* had carried on from there, whispering that Juliet Templeton's dark hair was just as Cudworth had described it, and that really, it was a wonder they hadn't guessed it themselves, given her mother's reputation.

Whispering that *Juliet* Templeton was the Lady in Lavender.

For a single, suspended pulse of his heart, Johnathan had even believed it himself, but then it had crashed into its next throbbing beat, sending a hot surge of blood into his veins, and his heart had known it for the lie it was.

Only one lady had ever found her way inside

those hallowed chambers, and it wasn't Juliet Templeton.

It was Emmeline. Emmeline, with her gray-blue eyes and soil-streaked pinafores, Emmeline, with that abominable silly lace cap, her rose petals and perfumes, and that mind of hers, as sharp as those wicked thorns on blasted Baronet Hume's Blush Tea-Scented China roses.

Ridiculous name, for a rose. Much too long. That Johnathan even remembered the whole of it was a testament to how deeply he'd fallen in love with her. He remembered everything about her. Her smile, her laugh, every word she'd ever spoken to him.

Perhaps he and Emmeline were a curious match, at least from a distance. Certainly, they were so to the *ton*, who were too preoccupied with fortunes and titles to care much for love, and lacked imagination when it came to marriage.

They'd put him with Lady Christine, for God's sake.

They were, however, far more imaginative when it came to scandal. To the *ton*, Juliet Templeton was just the sort of bold, vivacious beauty who'd catch the eye of an earl, and tempt him to abandon his duty to his mother and his title. That was a rumor they could feast on for weeks, at least until the end of the season.

To them, Juliet Templeton as a devious, ruinous siren made perfect sense, but when had love ever made sense? It was a tangled, messy business, painful and glorious at once, just like the Baronet's roses with their lovely scent, and deceptively innocent-looking thorns—

"Good morning, my lord."

Johnathan looked up from his teacup as his butler, Williams, entered the breakfast room, a silver tray with a stack of letters on it balanced on his hand. "Good morning, Williams. You may as well take the letters to my study, as I won't have time this morning to—" He paused as he caught a glimpse of the letter sitting on the top of the pile, his name scrawled on the front in Cross's bold script. "Was Lord Cross here, Williams?"

"Yes, my lord, an hour or so ago."

"So early? And he declined to stay?" That wasn't like Cross, who often had breakfast with him in the morning.

"Yes, my lord. He asked that you beg his pardon, and bid me give you the letter."

Johnathan took it from the tray, his chest tight. "Thank you, Williams. You may go."

"Yes, my lord." Williams bowed himself out as Johnathan tore open the letter and scanned the two sentences on the page before dropping the paper onto his plate, a frown on his lips.

Cross had gone off to Oxfordshire, to his hunting estate near Albury.

It wasn't wholly unexpected, as Cross had for years hosted a house party during the first two weeks of grouse season, but his departure seemed rather sudden, given he hadn't said a word to Johnathan about leaving London.

He read the two brief sentences again, but Cross had said only he'd see Johnathan with his new bride at Albury in two weeks' time.

His new bride...

There'd been a moment last night, right before

Johnathan had admitted he wasn't certain Juliet wasn't the Lady in Lavender, when Cross had seemed to be holding his breath, as if Johnathan's reply would make him the happiest of men, or shatter his world forever.

Cross had never been one to share the inner workings of his heart—indeed, most of the ladies in London would claim he didn't have a heart at all—but that expression on his face...

Johnathan had been too distraught to make any sense of it at the time, but now, looking back, he recognized the look for what it was.

Hope, right before it collapsed into the darkest despair.

But Cross, and Juliet Templeton?

The two of them hadn't ceased bickering since the moment they met. Cross contradicted every word out of Juliet's mouth with his usual arrogance, and when Juliet wasn't needling Cross, she was laughing at him. Still, when they were together, they were wholly focused on each other, and Johnathan had never seen Cross as animated as he was when he was in Juliet Templeton's company.

Yes, he quite liked them together. A tentative smile crossed Johnathan's lips, but it turned to a frown again as he glanced down at the open letter in his hand.

Had Cross fled London with hardly a word because he'd feared Johnathan was on the verge of making Juliet Templeton the Countess of Melrose? It certainly looked like it.

He dropped his head to his fist with a groan. Another proof that affairs of the heart were messy, tangled, and painful, especially when one threw passion into the mix.

For as long as Johnathan had known Cross, he'd been determined to avoid love entirely, but it seems it had found him at last, sometime between his first glimpse of Juliet Templeton's face, and their battle over *Romeo and Juliet*.

As for Johnathan, his heart was as permanently taken as Cross's appeared to be.

Well then, there was only one thing left to do. He tossed the letter aside, set his teacup on the tray, and left the breakfast room, calling to Williams to fetch his coat, hat, and stick, and order the carriage brought round.

It was time to put this business to rights, once and for all.

"GONE?" Johnathan stared blankly at Lady Fosberry, certain he must have misheard her. "Emmeline is *gone*?"

He didn't realize he'd raised his voice until Lady Fosberry rose from the settee and closed the door of her private parlor with a quiet click. "Yes, I'm afraid so, my lord. I tried every argument I could think of to dissuade her, but Emmeline can be terribly stubborn, despite her delicate appearance."

Johnathan had no trouble believing *that*. "But where the dev—that is, where has she gone?"

"Back to Buckinghamshire, to Hambleden Manor, very early this morning, and against my wishes."

What, another defection? First Cross, and now *this*?

"Emmeline Templeton has an unfortunate habit of running away." Johnathan didn't intend to let her evade him that easily, however. Hambleden was only forty or so miles from London, and he'd go a great deal farther than that to have her back.

"I don't mind telling you, my lord, I had little hope of persuading her to come to London in the first place, but once she was here, I thought perhaps..." Lady Fosberry trailed off with a sigh. "Well, it hasn't worked out as I'd hoped it would."

"What had you hoped for?"

"Why, a marriage for Emmeline or Juliet, of course, or for both of them, if the thing could be managed. Their father, bless him, wasn't able to do much for them, and they're in rather tightened circumstances."

"How tight?" Johnathan asked grimly.

Lady Fosberry hesitated, then let out another sigh. "Tight enough their younger sister Helena has taken a governess position with the Marquess of Hawke. She left only days before Juliet and Emmeline agreed to come with me to London. I fear they'll lose Hambleden Manor next."

Johnathan had suspected the Templetons were in dire circumstances from the few things Emmeline had said about Hambleden Manor, but her younger sister, forced out to work? She'd never said a word about *that*.

He thought about the way Emmeline's face had lit up when she'd described her home to him, the affection in her voice when she spoke of her sisters, and a pang of regret pieced his chest for her.

I should never have let her slip away from me so easily last night—

"I'd buy the house for them myself, if they'd let me, but those girls are dreadfully proud, just as their father was." Despite the impatience in her voice, a fond smile drifted over Lady Fosberry's lips. "Too proud for their own good."

Johnathan nodded, but he was thinking of Emmeline, alone in Lady Fosberry's carriage on her way back to Buckinghamshire. He could feel her sadness lacerating his own heart, as if her despair was his as much as her own, and he couldn't bear it.

He had to fetch her, and the thing must be done at once—he was finished being gentlemanly about it. He wanted his lady, and he wanted her *now*. "I'm going to marry Emmeline, Lady Fosberry," he announced, without preamble.

"Well then, my lord, it seems we both want the same thing. The only remaining question is, how are we meant to go about getting it?"

Johnathan blinked. "Well, I thought I might go to Buckinghamshire, and ask her."

It seemed a perfectly logical next step to him, but Lady Fosberry shook her head. "You *did* ask her, my lord, and she refused you. She didn't say so, but I'm certain she left with the hope that once she'd gone, you'd forget her and marry Juliet."

"*Forget* her?" Johnathan stared at Lady Fosberry in amazement. "How could I ever forget her? And there's no question of my marrying Juliet. Juliet Templeton doesn't love me, and I imagine my being in love with her sister is rather a stumbling block for her."

Johnathan considered mentioning his suspicions about Cross's affection for Juliet, but decided against it. That wasn't his declaration to make.

"Oh, I'm well aware you're in love with Emmeline, my lord." Lady Fosberry's eyes were twinkling. "You gentlemen are a great deal less mysterious than you think you are. The trouble is the *ton*."

Johnathan huffed out a breath. If he never heard another word about the *ton*, it would still be too soon. "I don't give a damn what the *ton* thinks. If I did, I would have married Lady Christine Dingley."

"To be fair, my lord, you haven't had any reason to worry about the *ton*. You're the Earl of Melrose, so they'll forgive you anything, but they aren't quite so forgiving of others. It's been several years since Alice Templeton ran off to the Continent with Lord Bromley, and the *ton* hasn't let her daughters forget it for a single instant."

Of course. Of course, Lady Fosberry was right.

How could he not have seen it? It was all very well for him to defy them, but a lady who'd been as mercilessly attacked by the *ton* as Emmeline Templeton had would dread another scandal above all else.

"But Emmeline must realize that once she becomes the Countess of Melrose, the title will protect her family from the worst of the scandal? There will still be murmurs, but a marriage will quickly silence the wagging tongues. There's no need for her to worry about the *ton*."

"She doesn't worry for herself, my lord, but for her sister, and for good reason. A marriage between you and Juliet would silence the wagging tongues, certainly, but a marriage between you and Emmeline —the sister of the lady all of London believes to be the Lady in Lavender? That will make it a good deal worse, at least until the *ton* grows bored of it, or the truth comes out."

Johnathan considered this, then gave a reluctant

nod. "I understand her worry, but how can she even think of tossing aside her own happiness over a dislike of gossip?"

Because there was nothing less than her happiness at stake. For all that Emmeline had run away from him, fleeing London at the break of dawn, he knew she was as madly in love with him as he was with her.

He'd seen it in her face, in her gray-blue eyes.

"I'm afraid it's more than merely a dislike of gossip, my lord. Emmeline imagines her sister sent back to Hambleden Manor in disgrace to languish, never able to return to London again without the *ton* making her feel ashamed of herself."

Ashamed. Johnathan flinched at the word. That was how Emmeline had felt, these past three years. He knew it instinctively, without Lady Fosberry having to say a word.

"Juliet hasn't done anything wrong, Lord Melrose. Emmeline said this over and over again last night when she begged me to allow her to return home, and then again, this morning. I assure you she feels every bit of her error over this Lady in Lavender nonsense, and she isn't one to let her sister suffer for her mistakes."

"Of course not, but—"

"There's something else, as well." Lady Fosberry laid a gentle hand on his arm. "Perhaps you don't know this, but James Templeton died within a year of Alice Templeton abandoning the family."

Johnathan nodded. "Emmeline said as much the day we went to visit Lady Hammond's roses, after that scene with Lady Dingley and Lady Christine."

Lady Fosberry's expression hardened at the mention of the Dingleys. "You may be certain I won't forget or easily forgive the Dingleys' part in all of this, nor Lord Cudworth's. As for the Templeton sisters, they tend to regard their mother's scandal and father's death as two parts of the same tragedy. Intertwined, you see. Not rationally—I don't know that they even realize they see it thus—but in their hearts. Particularly Emmeline and Euphemia, the eldest."

"You know them very well," Johnathan murmured.

"I do. The more one knows them, the more one loves them—all five of them. Indeed, my lord, I tell you all this not to discourage you, but because I hope with all my heart you can talk sense into Emmeline, for her sake and your own."

"Thank you, my lady."

"Emmeline wants persuading, and I fancy you're just the gentleman to do it, but I do think you should know that a battle lies ahead of you."

"Never fear, Lady Fosberry." Johnathan managed a small smile as he rose to his feet. "I don't intend to give up until I *do* persuade Emmeline. We gentlemen may not be as mysterious as we think, but we're persistent."

Lady Fosberry smiled. "Well then, there's nothing more to say, is there? Go and fetch our sweet girl, Lord Melrose."

~

LADY FOSBERRY REMAINED in her private sitting room for some time after Lord Melrose took his leave, until she was roused from her thoughts by Juliet, who appeared at the open door. "Was that Lord Melrose?"

"It was, indeed. Come here, dearest." Lady Fosberry held out her hand with an encouraging smile. "Shall I ring for refreshments?"

"No, I'm not hungry." Juliet took her hand and let herself be drawn down onto the settee. She gazed out the window for some time without speaking, then she said, "Emmeline's gone back to Hambleden Manor, hasn't she?"

"I'm afraid so, but my dear girl, don't look so despairing. All hope isn't lost. Lord Melrose is going after her."

Another silence, then Juliet said in a small voice, "Emmeline is dreadfully stubborn, my lady. Do you think Lord Melrose will be able to make her see reason?"

Yes, of course. I'm certain of it...

Those and a thousand other assurances rose to Lady Fosberry's lips, but the truth was, she wasn't certain of anything. So, she said only, "I hope so, dearest. We'll have to wait and see."

Juliet nodded, then fell silent again, and this time she remained so for some time. "Did Lord Melrose mention...did he say anything about Lord Cross?"

Ah, Lord Cross.

Another gentleman in love, and one with even less idea what to do about it than Lord Melrose. Of all the gentlemen in London Juliet might have chosen to gift with her heart, Lord Cross might be the most hopeless of them all.

Yet there was something perfect about the two of them, all the same. The sun and moon shared the same sky, after all, and the world hadn't come crashing down upon them yet.

"No, dearest, he didn't mention Lord Cross."

Juliet nodded again, but there was no mistaking her forlorn expression, her uncharacteristic listlessness.

"Did you know, my love, that Lord Cross has a handsome hunting box in Oxfordshire? He hosts a house party there every year, so that he and all the other fashionable gentlemen can rush about the country and terrorize the poor grouse. I daresay he's gone off there, or will go, quite soon."

"Lord Cross may do whatever he likes, and welcome." Juliet gave a disdainful sniff. "It doesn't matter a whit to me."

"Of course not, dearest, but I've been invited to attend his hunting party, and I thought you might enjoy coming along. It's perfectly proper for you to attend with me as your chaperone, and I've been longing to leave behind the grime of London and venture into the bracing country air."

Juliet perked up visibly at this, some of the color returning to her cheeks. "A house party with Lord Cross and dozens of loaded pistols lying about? That *does* sound diverting."

Lady Fosberry laughed. "I thought you'd think so. Do you suppose Euphemia can spare you for another few weeks?"

"I'll write to her, but I'm certain she won't mind."

"You do that, dear. Lord Cross may be a trifle surprised when you appear at his country estate, but surprises are pleasant things, aren't they?"

"I've always thought so."

"Yes, and I daresay Lord Cross could do with more of them."

"I couldn't agree more, my lady. He's far too complacent as he is."

"It's settled then, dearest." Lady Fosberry nodded, a tiny, satisfied smile on her lips.

Yes, this plan would do. It would do very well, indeed.

CHAPTER
FOURTEEN

Hambleden Manor was much as Emmeline had left it. It shouldn't have surprised her, given she'd been gone just over a week, but it felt as if a lifetime had passed since then. The shabby old place with its worn carpets and smoking fireplaces would always be as familiar as it was dear to her, but somehow, it wasn't the same.

Her home hadn't changed, but Emmeline had.

"Will you go out and have a wander in Papa's garden today, Emmeline? No one has been out since you and Juliet left for London. The fresh air will do you good."

Emmeline had been staring down at the open page of her book without seeing it, but now she looked up to find Phee had laid aside her embroidery, and was gazing at her with poorly-disguised concern.

"It looks cold outside." Emmeline glanced out the window at the gray sky, and an involuntary shiver wracked her, bone-deep and chilling.

"A bit, perhaps." Phee wanted to say more, but she thought better of it, because she pressed her lips together without venturing another word.

What was there left to say? Emmeline had told Phee everything that had happened in London—

Almost everything.

She hadn't told her Johnathan had said he loved her, nor had she confessed she was in love with him. She hadn't told Phee she was afraid she'd made a terrible mistake, leaving London.

But Phee knew every other wretched, heartbreaking detail, from Emmeline's shocking lapse of propriety in Lady Fosberry's library to the rumors about the Lady in Lavender, and finally that awful night at Covent Garden Theater.

She hadn't spared herself, or made any attempt to excuse her own conduct, but Phee hadn't chastised her. She'd said very little, but the sadness in her eyes was harder to bear than a scold would have been.

Phee never said she'd warned Emmeline not to go to London, never reminded her that she'd cautioned both Emmeline and Juliet another battle with the *ton* would send one or both of them fleeing back to the safety of Hambleden Manor.

She hadn't needed to. Emmeline was here, wasn't she? That was proof enough Phee had been right from the start.

"I had a letter from Juliet this morning," Phee ventured, after a long silence.

Emmeline tried to convince herself she was hoping to hear news of a betrothal between Juliet and Johnathan—that is, Lord Melrose—but the painful plunge of her heart argued otherwise. "How, ah...how does she do?"

"She's well enough, I think. She intends to stay with Lady Fosberry for another few weeks so she might accompany her to a house party in Oxfordshire."

"Is that all?" Emmeline swallowed. "No other news?"

Phee kept her attention on her embroidery. "No. Well, she did say she wished you would have bid her goodbye before you left Hampstead Heath."

She hadn't bid Juliet goodbye because she'd known Juliet would try and stop her from going, and she didn't trust that she had the strength to resist her. "It was easier this way."

Phee remained quiet as she pushed her needle into the fabric stretched across her embroidery frame, then pulled the long thread out the other side. "Nothing about this has been easy for either of you, Emmeline."

Emmeline looked down at her hands. "No."

Silence fell, broken only by the crackle of the fireplace until Phee drew in a deep breath. "Perhaps you shouldn't have—" she began, then startled as Emmeline jumped to her feet. "Emmeline?"

"I think I will go and muck about in Papa's garden, after all. It's not as if it's going to get any warmer, is it?" Emmeline attempted a smile, but she could see by the way Phee flinched it was a poor effort, indeed. She didn't want to worry Phee, but she couldn't bear to talk about it. Not yet. It was like poking at a raw, bleeding wound. "I won't be long."

Running away again. It was becoming rather a habit.

It *was* cold, she discovered as she hurried down the pathway of cracked stones that bisected the tiny patch of grass and led to the walled garden beyond. Even colder than she'd anticipated, the brisk wind cutting through the worn material of her brown cloak and sneaking underneath her battered straw hat.

She rubbed her arms, the wind leaving a sudden chill in its wake that pulled goosebumps to the surface of her skin. The sky was filled with moody, fitful clouds, and she could taste the first bite of fall in the air.

The gate surrounding the walled garden was rustier than she remembered, and a small section of the stacked stone wall had collapsed, but it was the same beloved place Emmeline remembered.

Now she was here, though, she could only stare dumbly around her, uncertain what to do. This garden was nothing like Lady Fosberry's—there was no intimidating perfection to be found *here*—but instead of inspiring, the gnarled roots and mass of tangled weeds exhausted her in a way they never had before.

Would it ever give her pleasure again? Or would she think of Johnathan with every bloom she sniffed, every petal she caressed? Would his face continue to haunt her, his cornflower-blue eyes always at the edges of her mind?

She touched her hand to her mouth, recalling the soft drag of petals against her lips just before Johnathan had kissed her among Lady Hammond's roses, and knew she already had her answer.

She'd never come across the damask rose she needed to recreate her father's scent, despite having visited several of England's finest gardens and sniffed dozens of different roses, some of them quite rare. It must have been one of her father's hybrids after all, because if such a damask rose was still in existence, she would have found it.

There would be no perfume. That her father's scent had died with him was one of the more painful outcomes from her ill-fated trip to London.

Not the *most* painful, but one thorn among the dozens piercing her heart.

She stomped on a dry clod of dirt, felt it crumble under her boot heel, and wished it were as easy to crush her dark thoughts. She'd have a dreary time of it, indeed, if she persisted in indulging in self-pity. It wasn't as if the Templetons had gained nothing from their time in London. Once Juliet and Johnathan married—

Not Johnathan. Lord Melrose. I must start thinking of him as Lord Melrose.

Her heart gave a pitiful throb as the thorns sank deeper, tearing at the tender flesh, and she raised a hand to her chest to sooth the pang. Perhaps she wouldn't think of *that* just yet.

But it wasn't as if London had been all bad.

She smiled a little as she recalled Mr. Beale's enthusiasm for her father's scent, his surprise at her ability to differentiate the subtleties of fragrance. She'd planted and grafted and harvested petals by her father's side for so long she no longer thought of any of her skills as remarkable, but Johnathan had thought they were.

Perhaps she didn't give herself enough credit.

She could create her own scent, something like her father's, or perhaps even something of her own. She'd have petals from the Hambleden Glory as soon as it bloomed. Lady Fosberry would see to that, and she'd brought cuttings back to Hambleden Manor with her, so she might grow her own. One could hardly go wrong with such a stunning scent as a base note.

All she needed to do was find the scents to harmonize with it, and while that was far more difficult than it sounded, she'd done it dozens of times before. She could make use of her father's workroom, which needed only cleaning and organizing to set it to rights.

She pictured her father bent over the long table with a glass bottle in his hand, dark tufts of his hair sticking up in tousled wisps around his head. The familiarity of that picture, the memory of his dear face made her nose tingle, her eyes sting, but there was joy there too, slumbering still, but swelling with promise. How he would have loved to see her carry on his work! How he would have encouraged her, and how proud he would have been, had he been alive to see it.

He'd always been so proud of all of them, so delighted by them.

She glanced around at the crumbling wall, the rusted gate, the brown edges tarnishing the petals of the few roses that had bloomed while she'd been gone. The garden needed a great deal of work, but she had all the time in the world to devote to it, and she could begin slowly, one corner at a time.

She crossed over to the side of the garden where what remained of the roses made a weak attempt to bloom. There weren't many colors—one pink, a yellow, and there in the back corner an ordinary white, but it was something.

She sank to her knees at one end of the row and began to clear away the debris so she might see what she had, and soon she became lost in the familiar sensation of rich soil between her fingers, and the scent of green, growing things in her head. When she came back to herself hours had passed, she was streaked with dirt, and the light was fading as the sun meandered ever closer to the horizon.

She dropped back on her heels and drew the back of her grimy hand across her forehead. She'd discarded her hat some time ago, and she suspected there were leaves caught in her hair. If Lady Fosberry could see her now, she'd be horrified, but it had been so good to feel the earth working its way under her fingernails once again.

She was tempted to stay in the garden until the light was gone, but Phee would be pacing in front of the windows by now, wondering where she was.

On her way back toward the gate, Emmeline paused to have a look at the white rose in the corner of the garden that had somehow managed to bloom despite its shady location and poor soil. It was a common tea rose, nothing special about it, but it was one of the few in the garden that had blossomed, and Emmeline rather admired its spirit.

As she drew closer, a faint hint of spice tickled her nose, reminiscent of clove, or—no, not that, precisely, but something else. Cinnamon? No, it was earthier than that, more like...

Ginger.

Emmeline froze where she stood, a wild rush of hope surging through her.

An everyday tea rose?

This humble little rose—not one of her father's rare hybrids, or the Portland rose, or one of Lady Hammond's damasks—was the rose she'd been searching for? Not a rare specimen at all, but just an ordinary rose one might find in any garden, anywhere in England?

No, it couldn't be...

But knowing her father as she did, it made perfect sense. He'd never been a high-stickler when it came to his roses. He'd loved them all, thought them all equally beautiful and worthy, from the Hambleden Glory to the damasks, and the damasks to the humblest tea roses.

She'd always believed she shared his impartiality, but if that was the case, why had she never once even considered the second rose in her father's scent could be a common hybrid tea? How many times had she passed this rose in the garden, without ever suspecting it was the elusive rose she sought?

Dozens of times. Hundreds, even.

Just a common little tea rose, unremarkable, easily overlooked...

But now she'd noticed it, truly *looked* at it, she saw it wasn't any of those things. It was lovely, with its pure white petals and its unique scent, and a hardy, courageous little flower, only unremarkable to those who expected it to be something other than what it was.

Some might think it not special enough to earn a place among Lady Finchley's roses, not exalted enough to bloom alongside Lady Hammond's damasks, but every rose was welcome in her father's garden. It would have been just like him to pair a humble tea rose with the extravagant, showy Hambleden Glory.

She raised a hand to her mouth, a sob on her lips, and reached out a shaking hand for one of the cheerful blooms. With a gentle twist she plucked it from its stem, buried her nose in its whorl of petals, and inhaled. The warm scent of ginger flooded her nose, citrus and wood and spice, so lovely, and so perfectly, unashamedly itself.

The rose she'd spent all these weeks searching for had been in her garden all along, just waiting for her to take notice of it—

"I've never known another lady who adores dirt as much as you do, Emmeline."

She went still, everything but her heart, which surged into sudden life, soaring in her chest on a wave of fierce happiness unlike any she'd ever felt before.

"How many of those pinafores do you have? I've been wondering."

She was afraid to turn around, or even to breathe lest he disappear like the sun now sinking below the horizon. Behind her came the clatter of the wrought iron gate opening, then the soft thud of booted feet crossing the garden.

"I'd suggest that a pair of gardening gloves wouldn't go amiss, but I prefer you as you are. I never would have guessed I could find dirt so fetching, but there it is."

He didn't sound angry, or frustrated that she'd fled London like a coward, but gentle and teasing and...happy, as if he'd found everything he'd been looking for, everything he'd ever wanted.

As if *she* was everything he'd ever wanted.

Her heart, so heavy just hours before, leapt with unrestrained joy in her chest. Her knees trembled, her entire body sagging with gratitude and relief, and she couldn't—she simply *couldn't* make herself send him away.

How had she ever thought she could give him up?

"Do you know, this is just how I imagined this moment would unfold?" The footsteps moved closer. "With you in that dreadful cloak, covered in dirt, with leaves in your hair, and me, thinking you're the most beautiful lady I've ever seen."

A sob caught in Emmeline's throat.

"Turn around, Emmeline." He was standing very close now, close enough she might have leaned into him, and found herself in his arms.

"Emmeline. Look at me, sweetheart."

She did as she was bid, because she could do nothing else. She turned and looked up at him, at his handsome face cast in shadows, the waning light behind him gilding him with a hazy silhouette of gold.

He studied her without speaking, then with a quick smile he reached out and plucked a leaf from her hair. When he met her gaze again his lips were still curved, but his eyes were serious. "You must have known I'd never let you go, Emmeline."

Had she? She wasn't sure of anything anymore, except that she loved this man with all of her heart, and he was *here*, he'd come for *her*, and nothing in her world would ever be right without him. "I—I don't know, or I didn't...understand, at first."

"And now? Do you understand now, sweetheart?"

"I think so," she whispered, giving him a shy smile.

He smiled back, his blue so warmth, and then in the next breath he was kissing her, his lips gentle and desperate at once, parting eagerly over hers, his tongue darting out to tease and coax her mouth open, a low groan rumbling in his throat when she did so at once, welcoming him inside.

He cupped the back of her head, all restraint gone as he kissed her over and over again, pulling her closer so not even a breath of air separated them, his heat chasing the chill from her skin, his long fingers tangling in her hair.

They were both breathless when he relinquished her mouth at last. "You won't ever leave me again?"

"No, never."

He stroked the backs of his fingers down her cheek. "I'm madly in love with you, Emmeline Templeton. I loved you before I ever saw your face."

Emmeline traced her fingertips over the strong line of his jaw before she took his face in shaking hands, her heart overflowing. "And I've loved you since our first moments together in Lady Fosberry's library, before I ever knew your name."

Johnathan turned his head to press a kiss to her palm. "You'll marry me, then?"

He looked so uncertain, yet at the same time so hopeful, she couldn't help but press another kiss to his lips. "I will, yes."

"Even if it means becoming a countess?"

Emmeline bit her lip to hide her smile. "Only if it means becoming *your* countess."

"Ah, that's lucky, then, because it does."

He took her mouth again then, his hands on her waist urging her closer, his lips parting on a groan as they opened over hers. She met him with shy caresses of her own, her tongue growing bolder with every dizzying stroke until things might have gotten quite heated, indeed, if she hadn't accidentally poked his chin with the stem of the white tea rose still clutched in her hand.

"What's this?" He reached out to finger a leaf. "Something new?"

"No." She smiled, shaking her head, and raised the bloom to his nose. "Something old. Do you like it?"

He caught her wrist, the cornflower-blue eyes she loved so well widening with surprise as he inhaled the intoxicating scent of wood, citrus, and warm spice. "That's lovely." He cocked his head as he examined the blossom. "Surprising little flower, isn't it? I wouldn't have put such a memorable scent with this rose, but of all the roses we've seen, this one is my favorite."

"It's special, isn't it?" Emmeline twined her arms around his neck, her heart swelling with love, and her head spinning with the scent of wild ginger. "It's my favorite, too."

EPILOGUE

Something was tickling Emmeline's back, brushing her spine and making her arch and shiver. She might have mistaken it for Johnathan's fingertips or his lips, as he often woke her with teasing caresses, but the touch was cool, and slightly damp.

It felt like...

"Is that a rose?" she murmured sleepily, a smile curving her lips. "Are you tickling my spine with a rose, my lord?"

"Mmmmm." The warm drift of Johnathan's breath fanned over the loose waves of hair tumbling in wild disarray around her face, and she could feel the warm press of his bare skin against hers.

"Which rose is it?" Her eyelids dropped closed as the wicked caress continued, gliding over the dip in the middle of her back before inching sideways to follow the curve of her waist. "It has a divine scent."

"It's the Lady Emmeline."

Emmeline opened one eye. "The Lady Emmeline? There isn't a rose named the Lady Emmeline that I know of."

"There is now. Margaret, Harriet, and Sarah have renamed the Great Maiden's Blush the Lady Emmeline, in your honor. They said it has the sweetest scent of any rose in the garden, and so it should be named after the sweetest countess in all of England. I could hardly argue with that logic, could I?"

A laugh bubbled up in Emmeline's throat. "*They* said so, or *you* did, and they agreed with you?"

"Hmm. I can't quite remember." Johnathan traced her earlobe with the rose, a soft laugh leaving his lips when she caught her breath at the caress. "But we all agreed the Great Maiden's Blush will hereafter be known as the Lady Emmeline, at least in the Melrose House gardens."

"Dear, sweet things." Emmeline had been apprehensive about meeting Johnathan's younger sisters, but she needn't have been.

All three of them had been crowded onto a window seat the day Johnathan brought her home to his country estate, their noses pressed to the glass. Her foot had hardly had a chance to touch the gravel drive before they burst through the front doors and gathered around her, chattering excitedly, each of them asking a dozen questions at once.

They were so like her own sisters Emmeline had felt instantly at home with them. Since then, what had begun as an eagerness on both sides to think the very best of each other had blossomed into a deep, genuine affection.

"Harriet and Sarah have declared they intend to become botanists themselves. As for Margaret, she's bursting with excitement over Tilly's visit next week, and has talked of nothing else."

"I wish we could have persuaded Phee to come," Emmeline said with a sigh.

Phee had been astonished to find the Earl of Melrose in the cramped entryway of Hambleden Manor the day he'd arrived to claim Emmeline. Her shock had quickly turned to quiet joy, but for all Phee's happiness for Emmeline, she'd so far resisted a visit to Kent.

"Give her time, love. She'll come, when she's ready."

In her worst moments, Emmeline worried that Phee would never be ready, that she'd spent too much time hiding at Hambleden Manor to ever willingly leave its secure embrace. She understood the urge to hide, the need to feel safe, but there was a great deal more to life than safety. Love, laughter, passion, hope —she wanted all of those things for all of her sisters —but sometimes she worried Phee would never give herself a chance to have them.

Johnathan, who could always tell when Emmeline was fretting over her sisters, shifted closer to her side, sliding one long, bare, hair-roughened leg between hers.

Ah, now *that* was Johnathan's mouth. There could be no mistaking those full, soft lips, open and demanding, the warm tip of his tongue tracing the line of her neck for any species of rose, no matter how divine.

"Turn over, my lady," he whispered in her ear.

Another delicious shiver skittered down Emmeline's spine as she wriggled onto her back, her cheeks heating just a little as Johnathan's gaze roved over her, the desire in his eyes warming every inch of bare skin it touched.

"Dear God, that blush drives me mad." He followed the rose as he teased it down her throat, his eyes darkening as he let it rest between her breasts. "The creamy white petals with the hint of pale pink are just the same color as your skin when you blush."

He traced the rose down her abdomen, pausing to tease her belly button with the impossibly soft petals before he drifted lower still, his blue eyes glittering as he dragged it over the slight curve of her lower belly.

Emmeline's blush deepened, and Johnathan's mouth curved in a slow, lazy smile. "Still so shy, after all these weeks as my countess?"

"It's not shyness, my lord." That wasn't entirely true, as there was a part of her that would always find her handsome husband's desire astonishing, but that rush of color to the surface of her skin had more to do with her consuming desire for Johnathan than it did with maidenly bashfulness.

"No?" Johnathan moved the rose back up her body to circle one taut nipple, his hot gaze darting to her face when a soft, breathless cry left her lips.

She swallowed at the breathtaking sight of him hovering over her, with his tousled golden hair and sensuous lips, his powerful chest and hard, flat stomach.

How amazing, that any man could be so handsome, and that that man could be *hers*...

But he *was* hers, body, heart, and soul. Since that fateful night in Lady Fosberry's library, Johnathan had shown her in a thousand different ways that his love belonged to her, and her alone.

"Tell me what it is, then, sweetheart," he crooned as he drew the rose across her chest to torment her other nipple, stroking and teasing until she was squirming against the bed, soft whimpers falling from her lips.

"Shall I show you, instead?" Emmeline closed her fingers around his wrist and pressed his hand against her body.

Johnathan's eyes burned, his lips parting further as she guided his hand to the warm, wet place between her thighs. He let out a low, tortured groan at the evidence of her desire, then tossed the rose aside, his game forgotten as passion overwhelmed them both.

There were no more words after that—just his hot, demanding mouth on hers, his tongue sliding between her lips to take her, stealing every thought from her head but the delirious pleasure of his touch, his quickened breath, his hungry mouth devouring hers, and his hoarse groans as his powerful body moved inside her, hard and hot, stroking so deeply Emmeline was lost to him, gasps tearing from her throat until with one deep thrust, he sent breath-taking waves of pleasure shuddering through her.

He held her close afterwards, murmuring drowsily, words of love and passion as he pressed tender kisses to her temple, her lips, the slowing pulse at the base of her throat. She stroked her fingertips over his back, through his damp hair, a smile that belonged to him alone on her lips.

They dozed in each other's arms for a while, Emmeline sure she'd never before been as warm as when she was in his embrace, until at last he stirred, and dropped a playful kiss on the tip of her nose. "I have something for you, my lady."

Emmeline shook her head, but her smile was dreamy. "Not another gift?"

Johnathan knew she didn't care much about silks or jewels or other extravagant trinkets, but he insisted it gave him pleasure to surprise her, so she'd ceased protesting, though occasionally she teased him about his countess being the most elegantly-dressed botanist in England.

"A gift for you to wear the next time we're in London." Johnathan fetched a square box of lovely, heather-colored velvet from the table beside the bed. "The *ton* must have *something* to gossip about."

There was still a great deal of talk in London over the Lady in Lavender. There were those who steadfastly maintained it was Juliet, while others claimed it had been Emmeline all along. Still others insisted that Lord Cudworth and Lady Christine—now Lady Cudworth—had fabricated the entire story, and there was a small but shrill contingent who would tell anyone who listened that Emmeline had bewitched poor Lord Melrose with a mysterious perfume, an elixir of roses that made him fall madly in love with her.

There were even some who whispered there'd been a wager between Lady Fosberry and the Templeton family over an ingenuous matchmaking scheme the Templeton sisters had invented, but Lady Fosberry had maintained a strict and uncharacteristic silence on that subject, much to the *ton*'s disappointment.

The only thing they all seemed to agree on was that Lord Cudworth was a great fool who couldn't distinguish one color from another, and Lady Christine a spiteful gossip.

Emmeline didn't pay much attention to any of it. She and Johnathan had spent little time in London since their marriage, preferring to remain on their quiet estate in Kent. So, it was easy enough for her to let the *ton* wear themselves out speculating.

She did, however, find it amusing they'd all so readily forgiven her for her part in the Lady in Lavender scandal, but they had their own reasons for choosing to so generously overlook her shocking behavior.

Simply put, the *ton* was mad to get their hands on the Countess of Melrose's infamous perfume, and since she was said only to give it away to her friends, all the *ton* was now clamoring to become Lady Melrose's dearest friend.

Of course, they had it all wrong, just as they usually did. Emmeline had never given that perfume to a single soul. Not to her friends, and not even to her sisters.

That scent belonged to Johnathan alone.

He laid the velvet box on the pillow between them. "Indulge me. This one is...special."

He opened the lid, and there, nestled in a bed of white silk was a parure, simple but heartbreakingly lovely. "Oh, my goodness." Emmeline reached out a hesitant finger to touch one of the dozen amethysts that made up the necklace. "Oh, it's beautiful. I've never seen anything like this."

The stones had each been intricately cut to resemble the petals of a rose, then inlaid with tiny, sparkling diamonds made to look like dew. They flashed with deep purple fire in their setting of delicate silver filigree leaves.

"I had it made for you." Johnathan took up the necklace and draped it around her throat, his blue eyes going so soft at the sight of the jewels dangling around her neck that Emmeline couldn't scold him for the extravagance of the gift.

She pressed a hand to his cheek, her throat tight. She didn't know what she'd done to deserve such a man, but fate had put them together in defiance of science, logic, even rationality, and who was she to argue with fate?

"Madame Toussaint is creating a gown to match the jewels." Johnathan brushed a stray lock of hair from her face with tender fingers. "Amethyst silk."

Emmeline smiled. "Not lavender?"

"No. Amethyst, of a very particular shade, and the only one of its kind, so you'll never again be mistaken for another lady." Johnathan took her hand and pressed a sweet kiss to her fingertips. "There is now, and will always ever be, only one Lady Emmeline, Countess of Melrose."

AUTHOR'S NOTES

Clifton, Mark. Nine Great Books on the Science of Love: The Mathematical Equation for "Happily Ever After" and Other Data Driven Revelations. CBC Life, February, 2020. https://www.cbc.ca/life/culture/9-great-books-on-the-science-of-love-1.5460947.

Ebeling, Jennifer. Margaret Cavendish Bentwick: The Portland Rose. The Daily Gardener Podcast. Maplegrove, MN. February, 2021. https://thedailygardener.org/ota20210211/ .

Fry, Hannah. The Mathematics of Love: Patterns, Proofs and the Search for the Ultimate Equation. TED Books, Simon & Schuster, New York, 2015.

Georgians: Parks and Gardens. English Heritage. https://www.english-heritage.org.uk/learn/story-of-england/georgians/landscape/.

J. Floris, perfumer, Jermyn Street, London, Atkinson's, Eonia Works, Southwark Park Road, Rotherhithe, London. *The British Perfumer* in 1822, by Charles Lille. Yardley's of London.

Shakespeare, William. *Romeo and Juliet*, 1597. Oxford: published for the Malone Society by Oxford University Press, 2000.

Thane, Anna. Cultivated Roses: A New Craze Begins. Regency Explorer. October, 2010. https://regency-explorer.net/roses/.

Whateley, Thomas. *Observations on Modern Gardening. G. Stafford, for T. Payne, London, 1793.* https://www.google.com/books/edition/Observations_on_Modern_Gardening/1tcxAQAAMAAJ?hl=en&gbpv=1&pg=PP9&printsec=frontcover.

ALSO BY ANNA BRADLEY

ABOUT THE AUTHOR

Anna Bradley writes steamy, sexy Regency historical romance—think garters, fops and riding crops! Readers can get in touch with Anna via her webpage at http://www.annabradley.net. Anna lives with her husband and two children in Portland, OR, where people are delightfully weird and love to read.

www.ingramcontent.com/pod-product-compliance
Lightning Source LLC
LaVergne TN
LVHW031449100225
803390LV00049B/1088